COBBLE BAY – THE VISITOR

AF408516

BY: Sandra Capwell

PROLOGUE:

Abby sat watching Shawn as he enjoyed the fire with Nutmeg curled up in his lap fast asleep. She was thankful for the life she was living with Shawn by her side.

He had brought love and peace to her in so many ways. When they met months before her days were full of grief over the passing of her friend George. His death had been a shock to everyone in the town of Cobble Bay.

Shawn came into her life when she needed someone to care for her. Since their meeting had saved her life, she learned every day how important he was to her.

Her family had accepted him into their lives. Cassie was so pleased that her mother had a man who was loving and protective. It had been more difficult for Henry. He did not relinquish the position of man in her life easily. When his sister made him realize what a good man Shawn was and the love he gave their mother, he decided to concede.

Abby was so pleased with how well the antique shop was doing since she had taken ownership. The steady flow of customers was bringing a good income. She loved going to work every day. Not only because she enjoyed the shop but working with Shawn by her side was the icing on the cake.

Abby had no way of knowing what the future had in store for her and Shawn.

CHAPTER ONE:

The weather had started to turn nasty. Abby could hear the wind and the rain hitting the window in the den. She was glad that Shawn had suggested closing the shop early.

After dinner, Shawn had brought in another load of firewood. "This storm might knock out the power. No harm in being prepared," he told her as he stacked the logs near the fireplace.

She walked over and set his mug of chocolate near his chair. As she sat down opposite him, she smiled as Nutmeg sat patiently waiting for Shawn to finish. Abby knew the cat would get comfortable in his bed near the fire when Shawn was done.

As they sat together watching the flames, Abby gave a silent thank you for the way her life had gone. It seemed longer than only months ago that everything had been completely different.

Before she met Shawn, she was mourning the death of her dear friend George. His tragic accident had been hard for the entire town to accept. He had been a resident of Cobble Bay for his entire life. Abby met him when she first walked into the antique shop. During the first months of her ownership of the shop he had been her mentor. She had learned so much from him about managing the shop.

After his death, a chain of events continued that brought not only physical but emotional trauma to Abby. With the appearance of Jefferson back into her life, Abby found strength that she was not aware she had. After his death, she was able to find peace.

"Where have you gone, my love?" Shawn asked. She turned to him and smiled. "Just thinking about how wonderful my life has been since you arrived." Before he could answer, the doorbell rang.

"Are you expecting anyone?" he asked. Abby stood to answer the bell, "I cannot imagine who would be out on a night like this." When she opened the door, she saw a boy standing on the porch. He was shivering and looked soaked through his clothes.

"Hi. Are you Abigail Sampson?" he asked. Abby nodded. "Yes, I am. Please come inside." She stepped back as he walked into the hall. "And who are you young man?" she responded to him. He stood shivering and watched as Shawn joined them in the hall.

"My name is Joseph Sampson, ma'am." He said. Abby could not hide her surprise at his answer. "Joseph Sampson Jr. to be exact." He added.

Shawn put his arm around Abby when he saw her reaction to the boy. She tried to understand how this was possible. Joseph only had one son and that was Henry. Before either of them could say anything to the boy, he started swaying and Shawn caught him as he started to fall. "Shawn, help him in by the fire. I will get a blanket." She went to the closet and grabbed an extra blanket for the boy. After wrapping it around his shoulders, she went to the kitchen and came back with a hot mug of chocolate for the boy. "This might help to warm you." She said as he took the mug into his shaking hands.

"Thanks. I got caught in the rain outside. Guess I was colder than I realized." He said to them as they both stood over him. Shawn took Abby's hand and led her to the sofa. While they waited for him to finish his drink, Abby tried to remain calm.

What was this boy implying? Did he expect her to believe that he was Joseph's son? That was not possible.

Or was it?

CHAPTER TWO:

The boy finished his chocolate and handed the empty mug to Abby. She walked to the kitchen and tried to compose herself before returning to the den.

"Well, I could see by your reaction that you did not know about me," he said to them. "No, Joseph. We did not. As you might expect I have questions for you." He nodded and waited for her to speak.

"The first thing I need is proof that you are who you say. Can you show me your birth certificate or identification?" Abby waited and watched as he dug through his backpack. She looked at the paper he handed her. It was, indeed, his birth certificate. It listed his father as Joseph Sampson and his mother as Maureen Bishop. He had been born in Old Orchard Beach almost nineteen years earlier.

Abby tried to understand how the boy could be Joseph's son. She thought about the date of his birth and how old her children were at that time. Henry was ten and Cassie was seven. Joseph had gotten his promotion at the hospital and was working long hours. Had he just told her he was working when in fact he had been with another woman?

Abby handed the paper back to the boy. Shawn took her hand. He tried to think of something to say that would help but could think of nothing. He could feel her hands trembling and he knew she was holding on to her emotions by a thin thread.

"Joseph or do you prefer Joe?" Shawn asked. The boy said Joe would be fine. Shawn looked at Abby. "Since it is rather late why don't we continue this conversation in the morning." Abby looked at him and smiled. He knew how difficult this situation was and how she was really trying to be considerate. "Yes, I think that would be a good idea too. Joe, do you have somewhere to stay tonight?" The boy looked at both and shook his head. "No, ma'am. I was going to look for a place, but it got too wet, and I wanted to see you before I lost my nerve."

She smiled at him, "Does your mother know that you were coming to see me?" He looked up and she could see tears in his eyes. "No. She told me about you last week. Just before she died."

Abby squeezed Shawn's hand. "Oh. I am sorry for your loss." She hesitated before continuing. "Joe. You can stay here tonight. We have an extra bedroom, and the weather is too stormy to look for lodging at this hour."

He smiled at her suggestion. "Well. If you are sure. That would be great. Thank you." Abby stood and said she would go up and get his room ready. Shawn watched her go up the stairs. When he was certain she was out of earshot he looked at the boy.

"Young man. I will say this only once. I love that woman. She is one of the kindest most loving people I have ever known. If what you are telling us is not the truth you will have to answer to me. Do you understand?"

The boy nodded. "Yes sir. My dad always told me she was a nice lady. He wanted to bring me to meet her someday. He died before that was possible."

Abby called from upstairs, and Joe went up to the bedroom. While she was showing him where the bathroom was, Shawn sat thinking about the boy's words. "Sounds possible, but there is something that just seems off about that young man." He thought. "I will definitely be watching closely before Abby gets too involved."

CHAPTER THREE:

Abby found it hard to sleep. Her dreams were full of Joseph. He was telling her something, but whenever she got close to hearing his words she would wake.

After tossing for hours, she decided to go downstairs. As she entered the kitchen, she saw Shawn sitting at the counter drinking coffee. "Well, looks like you had trouble sleeping also." She told him as she sat down.

He smiled and leaned in to kiss her softly. "Sorry. Did I wake you?" Abby shook her head. "Heavens no. My dreams were the reason I decided to come downstairs. Sleep was a lost cause."

He poured her a cup of coffee and they sat quietly with their thoughts. Shawn was not sure if he should voice the thoughts he had about Joe. He knew the boy's story sounded convincing. There was just something about him that affected Shawn's need to protect Abby.

Trying to make light of their new guest's appearance, "At least he is not a ghost." Abby looked at him and started to laugh. "Yes. We can be thankful for that." She replied.

Nutmeg wandered into the room. He rubbed against Shawn's legs and then Abby's. They watched as he walked over to the door. "Guess we disturbed someone else." Shawn said as he opened the door and watched the cat go outside.

Abby looked at Shawn, "What are your thoughts about Joe? I must admit I am slightly skeptical about his story. Showing up so late almost looked like he expected an invitation to stay the night."

Shawn nodded. He was glad she was having the same thoughts as he was. "Yes. I do tend to agree with you. I am trying to give him the benefit of the doubt, but it is not easy. Why didn't he contact you first before just showing up at our door? Especially last night in that storm."

Before she could answer a noise made her turn towards the hall. There stood Joe in the doorway. They both stopped speaking. He walked into the kitchen and stood by the counter.

"I know what you both must think of me. I am sorry that I came to your house so late. That is why I was so wet. I had been walking up and down the sidewalk in front for over an hour. My mother told me where you lived. She felt you should know that I existed. I understand you're not trusting me."

Abby looked at the boy and felt guilty about the thoughts she was having. "Joe. Please understand. I had no knowledge of your existence. Your father never gave me any reason to even consider he had another family. He told me he was keeping long hours at the hospital and that is what I believed. I had no reason to think otherwise."

Shawn watched Joe's face as he listened to Abby. He looked remorseful, but Shawn still had a gut feeling that he was not being honest with either of them.

"Why don't you sit down at the table with us Joe. I will make breakfast and we can start over. I would like to hear from you about your father. Did he stay with you and your mother often?"

Joe walked over and sat down at the table as Abby asked. Shawn followed him and waited for an answer to her question. "My father was not around very much. I can remember him appearing late at night and visiting us. He would sit on the floor with me and watch while I built with my blocks."

Abby tried to remember a time when Joseph had ever taken time to sit with Henry or Cassie while they played. He always was in a hurry to get to the hospital or too tired after working all day. He never paid either of them much interest after they were born. He would show attention on the rare occasions that anyone visited.

She always thought that he only put on an act in front of others. She knew he did not show any interest during her pregnancies. He made her feel like she was someone to hide when she became huge during the final months before giving birth. She stayed in the house as much as she could.

Now to hear that he had been attentive with Joe as a child brought tears to her eyes. She tried to hide her feelings as she prepared the bacon and eggs. When she felt Shawn's arms around her, she knew he understood her emotions.

As they sat and ate their food, Joe only glanced at Abby and Shawn. He ate like he had not had a meal in days. "Where have you been living since your mother passed," Abby asked.

"I had a friend that let me sleep on his sofa," he answered with his mouth full of food. "The landlord had evicted me after my mother went to the hospital. He knew I would not be able to pay the rent. We already owed him months back rent that my mother had not been able to pay. After my father died the money stopped coming from him. My mother worked as a server at night, but when she got real sick, she had to quit her job."

Abby listened and tried to imagine what life had been for this young man. First his father died and left them without income. Then his mother gets sick and dies. He lost not only both of his parents, but his home as well. "Joe. I am sorry for what you have had to go through during the past few months. I cannot even imagine how hard it has been for you. When you finish eating, I would like time to discuss the situation with Shawn. If you could go for a walk, we will let you know what decision we have come to about helping you."

He ate the rest of his food. When he took his dishes to the sink, he got his coat and walked outside. After stopping to rub Nutmeg's ears he walked out to the street and down the sidewalk.

Shawn sat and waited for Abby to explain her thoughts. She knew she wanted to help this boy, but he could not help to think it would lead to heartache for her. He just was not sure why he felt that way.

Abby sat down next to Shawn. He could see the hurt in her eyes as he reached for her hand. "I can see how torn you are about this boy. The only advice I can give is to be careful no matter what you decide. We have to be vigilant. You do not know anything about his story."

Abby nodded in agreement. She could not help but feel compassion for Joe. He had lost so much. She felt guilty for everything her children had during the years they shared with her. Joseph might have been absent, but they always had her love and support. This boy seemed to have had neither.

CHAPTER FOUR:

Joe walked down the sidewalk away from Abby's house. He pulled his phone out of his pocket. "Hey. Yes, I arrived last night. She let me stay in the house because of the storm. I know, I am working on her slowly. She seems open to my story. I am just walking around while they discuss what comes next. I will call you in a few days. Just be patient. I am sure everything we planned will happen. You just have to be patient."

When he turned back towards the house, he could see Abby on the front porch waving. As he got closer, he could see her smiling at him. "Yes, it looks like she has come to a decision in my favor," he thought.

Joe smiled and waved back at Abby. When he reached the porch, she waited for him to come inside. "Joe, come into the den. Shawn and I would like to talk to you." He followed feeling hopeful that they had decided to allow him entry to their lives.

When they were all settled in the den, Abby began. "Joe, we have discussed everything you told us last night and this morning. I am sorry for the way your life has gone in the past few months. It was a total surprise to meet you. Your father never gave me any hint about you or your mother. That, however, is in the past. Shawn and I agree that we would like to try and make a brighter future for you. It will take time for us both to trust you, but we are willing to try."

Joe listened and tried to control his pleasure. He had been told of how compassionate this woman was. His research into her and her family gave him all the information he needed to find a way into her life.

As he spoke, he even managed tears to give his response more impact. "Ma'am. I am so thankful for the compassion you have shown me. I promise to try very hard to convince you and Shawn that I am being honest. I just want to know you and find myself a better life."

Abby reached over and took his hand. "Joe. You have a place here with us for as long as you need. There is an extra room over the garage that was used by our caretaker many years ago. We can clean it and make it more livable. It is yours if you want." He nodded in answer to her offer.

Shawn sat and did not add anything to the conversation. He was watching every movement and hearing every response from the boy. He saw the tears but did not believe they were sincere. "This boy is hiding something, and I will discover what regardless of how long it might take. In the meantime, he will definitely be on my radar."

Joe looked over at Shawn and smiled. The look that was returned was puzzling. He knew he would have to work harder for Shawn to come around to his presence.

CHAPTER FIVE:

Abby asked Shawn to take Joe to the garage. While they were gone, she called Cassie. "Hi Mom. How are you?" Abby took a breath, "Hello sweetie. How are you feeling?" Cassie said she was great. After a few moments Abby spoke. "I wondered if you had time to visit. Shawn and I have someone we want you to meet." Cassie said she would ask Jake if they could get away. "I will call you back Mom. Is everything all right? You sound a little strange." Abby did her best to convince her daughter that everything was just fine.

After she hung up, Cassie turned to Jake. "That was Mom. She wants us to come for a visit. She said there is someone they want us to meet." Jake listened to his wife. "Who could that be? Maybe a relative of Shawn. Maybe they have decided to make their partnership permanent." She smiled. "I only hope that is the reason. However, my "spider sense" says there is more to it than just a simple proposal."

After ending her call to Cassie, Abby called Henry and asked the same. "Well, Mom. I was planning on surprising you with a visit soon. It would be good to see everyone. Is Cassie and Jake coming?" She told him she was waiting for a callback from his sister. "Well, you can count on us. How about next weekend?"

They agreed on the date and Abby was pleased when Cassie called back saying the weekend would work for them also. She sat trying to think how she would explain to her children that they had a half-brother.

*****

Joe followed Shawn up the outside steps to the second floor over the garage. "Wow. My own entrance. That works," he thought to himself. When he walked inside, he saw a large space that was obviously being used for storage. "Might take some hard work, but I think this will work nicely for you Joe." Shawn told him.

"Yeah. It definitely will. I do not mind hard work. In fact, I could start clearing out the space now if that is ok with you." Shawn nodded and pointed out things that could be sent to the dump. As he worked alongside the boy, he was impressed on how strong he was. His appearance looked like a frail body, but Shawn found he had the wrong impression.

Abby joined the two men after a short time. She handed them each a bottle of water as she looked around the space. "Wow, I forgot just how much junk got thrown up here."

The three of them worked for hours and were pleasantly surprised at how much they done. They had uncovered an old iron bed frame that would work nicely. "All it needs is a new mattress. That dresser in the corner looks like it is still sturdy enough."

Shawn noticed how much more relaxed Abby looked. He knew she always felt better when she was helping someone else. He had seen it in the shop many times when she would discount items for customers that appeared needy.

He was glad she was taking her steps cautiously with Joe. "I will be interested to see the response from Cassie and Henry when they arrive. It might decide the course that Abby follows in Joe's future." He thought to himself.

CHAPTER SIX:

Abby and Shawn walked down the garage stairway. He took her hand at the bottom and pulled her in for a warm, deep kiss. Smiling they continued to the kitchen.

Joe stood at the top of the stairs watching the couple until they disappeared inside the house. He turned and walked back into the loft area. Looking around he realized this was twice the space he had in the apartment he shared with his mother. He knew his presence here had been planned by his mother for quite some time.

The money his father had given her ran out months after his death. She had gotten a job at the local diner and talked the owner into hiring Joe as a dishwasher. They worked side by side for months. He had finished high school when he was eighteen.

He would have long conversations with his mother. She told him what a wonderful, loving man his father had been. He had promised to leave Abby and marry her. Joe remembered the visits from his father. He was very attentive to both. His mother believed that they would be a family someday. All their money problems would be gone, and they would lead a happy and normal life.

When Joseph died, his mother had seen the obituary in the local paper. She wanted to attend his funeral but decided to wait before making her presence known to Abby. She started to formulate a plan when she read about the Antique Shop. She knew Abby had bought the shop with money she received from Joseph's will.

Maureen would lie awake at night worrying about their finances. Her anger and jealousy of Abby grew deeper every day. She resented the life Abby had with her children. She felt that life had been denied her and Joe.

When Maureen finally told Joe about her plan to get the life, she felt they deserved, he was hesitant. "Mom. We can manage without doing anything against Dad's other family." She would tell him they would only be taking what rightfully should have been theirs after Joseph passed away.

She knew Abby had stopped Joseph from any plans of leaving her. Maureen had made her mind believe Joseph was coming to her to make her his wife. She was certain that Abby had kept him home so she could reap the rewards when he died.

The more she dwelt on the subject night after night, she became a woman obsessed. Joe began to feel afraid of his mother. She would sit alone at night and make notes in a journal about what her plan was. It depended mainly on her son winning over the trust and affection of Abby. She would tell him every day about how wonderful life would be when they got what Joseph had intended for them.

Joe did not argue with his mother. He had come to realize that she was consumed by her grief over losing the love of her life. He knew she would not rest until she had taken everything from Abby. He also knew he had to follow her orders and fulfill her plan for their future.

After spending time with Abby, he started to have doubts about the mission his mother had given him. Even after only a few days with Abby, he felt what a warm, giving person she was.

He thought if his mother had only met her and talked to Abby, they could come to an arrangement. The way Abby was so concerned for the life he had said he had been living brought thoughts about confessing the truth.

Joe knew if he did that, there was no telling what his mother would do. To any of them.

CHAPTER SEVEN:

Abby was impressed by how much Joe had done in the loft. He was surprised with the delivery of a new mattress for his bed. "Wow, this is great. You really did not have to buy a new one." She smiled at his response. "Well, if you do not want it, we can call the store to return it." Joe looked at her and after a minute he realized she was only teasing him.

They laughed while he helped her make the bed with the new linens, she handed him. When she put the finishing touch on the bed with a large quilt she had, he could not wait to try it out. He sat down on the edge of the bed and Abby thought she saw a glimmer of a tear. She did not mention it so not to embarrass Joe.

"I am cooking a roast for dinner. It should be ready by six." She said as she walked toward the door. "Thanks. That sounds great. I am so thankful for all you are doing for me ma'am." She turned toward him and knew he was sincere by the look on his face. "Joe. You are family."

He sat on his new bed after she had closed the door. Her words rang in his ears. "Family." He could not understand the kindness she was showing to him. A perfect stranger to her. He knew Shawn did not totally agree with Abby. He still had his doubts about Joe. But, even Shawn was acting like he was a member of their family.

"I have to convince my mother about these people. She may have talked herself into believing otherwise about Abby." He thought as he stretched out on the big comfortable bed.

*****

Abby was in the kitchen peeling potatoes when Shawn came in from the back yard. He walked over and put his arms around her waist. She turned towards him and kissed his lips lightly. "What have you been up to?" she asked. "Just cleaning up the yard. Branches came down in the storm and I wanted to put them in a pile before they were covered with the snow."

He stood and watched as she prepared their meal. "The store delivered the mattress before." She told him. He nodded. "Yes, I saw the truck as it was leaving. Was Joe surprised?" She looked up and smiled. "Oh, yes. He actually teared up some. We put the sheets and quilt on the bed. When I left, he was stretched out, smiling."

"What are your plans for him? Have you given any thoughts about the future?" Abby walked over and sat down next to him. "I think I am going to suggest he come to work at the shop with us. We still have things that need painting. He can help with the remodel and that will free you up for customers."

Shawn listened and told her he agreed with her plans. Joe had shown initiative with the loft. He might prove to be an asset in the antique shop as well. He was not totally convinced that the boy was being honest about his situation. He hoped he was wrong. Abby had already taken the boy under her wing as if he was another son she had never met before.

"When are you expecting the kids to arrive?" he asked her. "I have not spoken to Cassie since the other day. I better give her a quick call after dinner to find out their arrival plans. That way I can be certain to have the meals covered. You know how much that crowd can eat."

They were laughing when Joe came in the door. "Hi. Can I do anything to help?" he asked them. Abby told him where the dishes were. He went to the cabinet and Shawn watched as he started to place the dishes on the kitchen table. "Is this where we are going to eat tonight?" Joe asked. Abby nodded and he continued his job while Shawn walked out to the den. He took his usual chair by the fire and ruffled Nutmeg's fur as the cat got comfortable on his lap.

Abby called him for dinner. "Well, sorry my furry friend. Time for me to eat. You can have your dinner after we are done. I bet I can find scraps for you." The cat sat on his bed in front of the fireplace. He knew by the smells there would be some extra good food tonight.

The dinner was as delicious as it smelled. Shawn told Abby what a great cook she was. "I second that," said Joe. "I have not had too many good meals lately. This one really makes up for the last few weeks." Abby thanked them both as they all enjoyed the roast. Shawn asked Joe more about his life growing up. Abby listened to his comments and found she was very glad this young man had shown up at her door.

She did worry about the meeting with Cassie and Henry. She knew her children were protective of her, but she hoped they would be accepting of Joe. He was, in fact, their half-brother.

CHAPTER EIGHT:

Abby left Shawn and Joe clearing the table. Shawn had told her to make her call while they cleaned up the dishes. She walked into the den and passed Nutmeg as he was rushing to get his dinner. She sat down near the fireplace and picked up her phone. As she hit the number for Cassie, she thought how anxious she was for her children to meet Joe.

"Hello Mom." Abby smiled at the sound of her daughter's voice. "Hi dear. Just checking in to see if we are still on for the weekend." Cassie assured her that they would be arriving early afternoon on Saturday. "I am so looking forward to your visit. Shawn is too." They talked for a short time and Abby said she had to call Henry. "Oh, you do not have to check with him," Cassie said. "I talked to him yesterday. They should be arriving around the same time on Saturday. He said he was curious about the visit. I have to admit. Jake and I are too. I hope everything is all right with you and Shawn." Abby told her that the visit was not about her or Shawn. It was just something that needed to be addressed in person. The call ended just as Shawn walked into the room.

"Everything all set for their visit?" he asked. Abby nodded and moved over so he could join her on the sofa. He put his arm around her and gave her a kiss as Joe walked in. "Oh. Sorry. Don't mean to intrude." He said to them. Abby just smiled.

"No problem. You have to get used to the love in this house." Shawn told the boy. Joe smiled. "It is nice to see how you both care about each other." He sat down on the floor next to the fireplace. He reached over to pet Nutmeg, but the cat walked away from the boy. Shawn thought that was strange as the cat jumped into his lap.

"Guess he prefers you," Joe commented. Shawn nodded and gave the cat a pat on the head. Abby laughed. "Nutmeg has become Shawn's constant companion even over me. He is slightly fickle I am afraid."

They sat talking for hours. Joe told them more about his mother and the life he remembered. He told Abby about the short visits they would have with Joseph. She listened and instead of feeling angry at her deceased husband, she felt sorry for the brief time he was able to spend with Joe.

Before Joe left for his room, Abby told him Cassie and Henry would be arriving on Saturday. He nodded and made no comments. She watched as he walked out of the kitchen door. Shawn checked the doors and followed her upstairs. "How did Cassie sound when you spoke to her?" he asked. Abby told him the children all seemed anxious about the visit. "I hope everything goes well. I know it will be a shock for them. It has been for me. I knew Joseph was distant, but I never imagined he had another family somewhere. I guess since he stopped being intimate with me, I just thought he was too absorbed with his position at the hospital. That was naïve on my part."

Shawn took her in his arms after she climbed into bed. "I cannot understand how he could look at another woman. The time we have spent together has shown me how loving and compassionate you are. How he could even consider leaving you and your children is beyond my comprehension. Not nice to speak ill of the dead. But I think he was a jerk."

Abby cuddled closer in his arms. "I am so glad I found you Shawn. I had a good life with Joseph. Well, in the beginning anyway. He was affectionate and caring. But he never made me feel the way I do with you. You make me feel safe and loved every moment. I love you so much."

He looked down at her. "I love you too Abby." He said as he began to caress her naked body. His fingers brought an immediate response from her. She reached for him, and he let out a soft moan. As they joined together Abby knew this was the man she was meant to be with. Her body responded to his every touch. He made her feel relaxed and safe in his arms.

They finally fell asleep, exhausted from their love making. Neither of them heard the kitchen door open as Joe walked softly into the house. He listened and when he was confident the house was quiet, he walked into the den.

Joe checked the drawers on the desk. He rifled through the papers he found inside. His mother had told him to find any bank statements he could find. She wanted to know what their financial situation was at the moment.

When he completed his mission and let himself back outside, he took his phone and called his mother. "Well, it is about time you called. I was beginning to wonder if you forgot the number." She said to him angrily. "Sorry. I had to wait until they were asleep. I checked the desk and found bank papers. You were right Mom. They are very well fixed financially." He went ahead to tell her about the numbers he had seen. He could tell by her voice that she was smiling.

"Well, sounds good. What about your living situation? Have you met her children yet?" Joe told her the garage apartment was suitable. He did not elaborate on how great it really was. He also told her about the weekend visit they were expecting from Abby's children.

After telling her that he would be in touch after the weekend, the phone call ended. There were no kind words from his mother. She never said that he was doing a good job. She just kept repeating the same thing. "Find out about all their finances. We want to be able to get everything that should be ours when your mission is done. Then our life can be the way your father promised it would be."

Joe would always agree with her, regardless of how his mind had changed since he met Abby. He knew he had to complete the job his mother had given him. He also knew how it would hurt Abby which was giving him second thoughts.

CHAPTER NINE:

The next day started with breakfast as usual. Abby and Shawn had discussed bringing Joe to the shop earlier before he walked into the kitchen. "Joe. We were thinking about bringing you to the antique shop today. We could use your help around the shop with painting. Shawn has finished some of the rooms, but there are places that need to be spruced up a bit. We have both been impressed by the incentive you have shown in the garage loft."

She waited for Joe to answer. He looked at both of them and started to smile. "Wow. That would be great. I was wondering how I could repay you both." Abby laughed. "This would be a paying job, Joe. We would start you out as a handyman around the shop. If that works out, you can help up with customer deliveries."

He nodded at her explanation. "I would really like that. The odd jobs I have had lately have not really been too good. I bet I could learn a lot from both of you. Thanks for taking a chance with me." He finished his food and carried his plate to the sink.

He turned to them, "let me know what time to meet you outside." Abby said they should leave in a half hour. He nodded and told them he would be outside when they were ready.

After he walked out the door, Shawn leaned over and kissed Abby softly on the lips. "What was that for?" she asked him. "Just showing how much, I love you, Abby Sampson." She blushed, "I think you did that quite nicely last night."

*****

Joe called his mother when he got back to his room. "Hi mom. Just wanted to check in with you." Maureen responded with multiple questions about his progress. "Everything is going according to your plan. Abby just told me they are letting me work in the shop with them starting today." She laughed. "Oh, now that they are allowing you to live there, they will be using your slave labor."

Joe was not surprised at his mother's words. He hesitated before he answered. "No. This will be a paying job. They are not just using me because of the room and food." Maureen's tone changed at once. "Joe. You sound like you are starting to like that woman and her man. I hope you are not having second thoughts about what we discussed."

"No mom. I am still sticking to the plan. Just trying to get closer so we can find a way to her money. Don't worry. I am still doing what you asked. There is no reason to doubt my loyalty to you." She told him that she hoped he would keep his guard up. "When are you going to meet her kids?" Joe told her that would be on the weekend. "I will call you after they leave." She seemed satisfied and ended the call.

Joe sat on his bed thinking about his mother. He wished she could see what a sincerely decent woman Abby was. He hated to admit even to himself that Abby had already shown him more attention than his own mother had for quite some time.

He grabbed his jacket and raced down the stairs. He actually was looking forward to working in the shop with Abby and Shawn. He knew he was supposed to be looking for any opening to get further into Abby's good graces. He did not want to think about the plans his mother had for the future.

Maybe he could convince her to see the situation differently. He felt if they could all meet and talk, the plans would not have to end so tragic for Abby. He did not want to think about helping his mother swindle Abby out of her money.

And he definitely was not prepared to help end her life.

CHAPTER TEN:

The drive into town was quiet. Joe sat in the back remembering the conversation with his mother. She was so determined to get all that Abby had received from his father. He knew she was hurt when she saw how prosperous Abby was after his father's death. He had loved his father and had fond memories of the brief moments they spent together as a family. Now that he was older, he realized his father had not been honest with Maureen. He had told her they would be together after he divorced Abby. Joe now felt his father never had any intention to divorce and leave his family for Maureen.

When they arrived at the shop, Joe tried to look surprised. He had of course seen the shop before. When he was young, he had traveled with Maureen to Cobble Bay. They had walked the streets in the small town. Maureen had let Joseph know of their presence and he had not been pleased with her surprise. He had not been able to make time for them, so they only spent a day in the town. He could remember visiting the antique shop with Maureen. They browsed through the shop while she waited for a phone call from Joseph. When he finally called to say he could not get away from the hospital, Maureen took her son back to their apartment.

When the notice appeared in the local paper about Abby becoming the new owner of the antique shop, Maureen was livid. She remembered how grand the shop appeared and she could only imagine the money Abby had to invest to become the owner. She felt it was money that should have been hers and Joe's after Joseph passed. Now with her son's help, she fully intended to re-claim her rightful inheritance.

Joe knew her anger would not be gone until she dealt with Abby in the most permanent way possible. That was a part of her plan that upset him the most. He had been in and out of trouble in his teens, but never anything so terrible as what his mother expected of him.

*****

"Well, Joe. What do you think about the shop?" Abby asked as they walked inside. He looked around and thought the furniture looked even grander than he remembered. "Wow. This is really something." He said to her. She smiled as they followed Shawn inside the office.

"Why don't you look around while I get today's deposit ready for the bank. Shawn will show you the projects we have planned." Joe followed Shawn into the back room. He listened while Shawn explained the areas that still needed painting. As they walked through the large showroom area, Joe could tell from his voice just how much the shop meant to Shawn.

"You have been working here with Abby for some time, right?" he asked. Shawn nodded in answer. "Yes, it started as just a part-time job last year during the winter months. The fishing boat I had been working on did not have enough business for their entire crew. I must admit taking this job was only partly for the money. Most of my interest in the shop was for Abby." Joe listened without commenting.

Abby walked past them and said she was heading for the bank. Shawn winked at her and continued the tour with Joe. "You really have a thing with Abby, huh?" the boy asked. Shawn stopped walking and glanced at her as she crossed the street. "We have become close during some very strange and dangerous circumstances."

Joe did not ask for any more details. He had heard some of the local gossip about the former owner. The newspaper in his town had carried the story about Jonathan's suicide from the roof of the shop.

He was curious about Shawn's comment but did not push for more information.

When they got near the attic door, Shawn stopped. "That is just the attic. Nothing to see up there for right now." He led Joe into the break room and the boy watched as he made the first pot of coffee for the day. Abby returned and found them sitting with their coffee.

"Well, what do you think Joe? Do we have a new part-time helper?" He smiled at her, "Yes ma'am. I am looking forward to getting busy. I promise to do my best to repay you for all your hospitality."

She walked into the office with Shawn as Joe picked up the paint can and headed to begin his first job. "What do you think Shawn? Am I making a mistake with Joe?" He looked into her big blue eyes and saw the caring woman that he loved so much. "No, I think Joe is going to work out just fine. He seems sincere in his promise to do a good job."

Abby reached up and gave him a quick kiss just as the first customer of the day entered the shop.

"Good morning. Welcome to Cobble Bay Antique Emporium. If you have any questions, we will be glad to help you." Abby told the couple. She watched from the office as they browsed through the room displays. She saw Shawn moving items around in the front windows to make room for Joe's painting project.

"This is the beginning of a great day," she thought to herself. "I think this young man is going to fit in with our family very well."

CHAPTER ELEVEN:

The day proved to be very busy. Shawn and Abby kept busy assisting customers. Joe was content with the projects that Shawn had given him. He was surprised when they walked over and told him it was time to take a break for lunch.

Joe followed Abby and Shawn across the street to the café. He sat quietly checking out the menu. After they had ordered their food, Abby asked Joe about his life with Maureen. They listened while the boy explained how his life growing up was not exactly what they expected. He explained about his difficulties as a teen. "I guess I just never fit in with the kids at my school. It was a tough neighborhood and there were a lot of gangs. I got in with the wrong group and did spend time in juvenile detention. My mother tried her best, but with the jobs she had working at night, there was just too much temptation to get into trouble." He looked at their faces and felt like he had said too much.

"Joe, I am sorry. I know what it is like to grow up without too many friends. It is easy to follow the wrong people." Shawn told him. Abby listened and did not say anything at first. "Now that you are here with us, I hope your life can turn around." She told the boy. He had expected a different response when she heard his story. "Thanks for the chance you have both given me," he said.

They sat quietly enjoying their lunch. Shawn felt remorse for the way he had judged Joe. He was open to changing his mind about the boy. However, there was still that feeling in his stomach that something was off about Joe's story.

They walked back to the shop and Joe returned to his painting while Abby and Shawn went to the office. "What are you thinking?" Abby asked Shawn. "I could see the look on your face when Joe was telling us about getting into trouble as a teenager." He nodded. "It just made me remember my younger days. I was not always the handsome and attentive man you see before you." She laughed at his answer.

"I find it hard to believe you were ever anything other than the man I fell in love with." He put his arms around her and just as he leaned in for a kiss, the bell rang on the door announcing a customer.

"Saved by the bell," she said as she walked out of the office. Shawn nodded and watched Joe as he was painting in the front display window. "Yes, I can definitely relate to Joe's explanation." He thought to himself.

The afternoon ended with quite a few new sales. Joe had taken his paint supplies into the back room as Shawn walked in to join him. "Good job today, Joe. The front display windows look really good. You seem to have a talent for painting. I can manage, but I am not as neat as you seem to be." Joe laughed and thanked him for the kind words.

Abby joined them and asked if they were ready to leave. Shawn nodded and started to follow her out the front door. Joe joined them on the sidewalk. "I think I am going to walk home. I want to stretch my legs and check out some of the other shops. Is that all right?" Abby agreed. "Dinner should be ready around six." He thanked her and said he might just pick up something in town.

Shawn was pleased to think he would have Abby to himself when they got home. He was not thinking about their dinner. More about dessert.

When they started to drive towards the house, she asked what he was smiling about. "Oh nothing." He responded.

Joe watched them as they drove away. He walked around the building and checked out the alley behind the shop. He stopped when the person stepped out of the shadows. "I saw you from the back room. What are you doing here mother?" he asked the woman standing in front of him. "What if they had seen you?"

Maureen walked over to him. "What if they had? They have no way of knowing who I am." She put her hand on his arm. "So, tell me about the shop. Were you able to see any books that showed their profits?"

He pulled away from her hand. "No. How would I with both of them right there." He replied. She looked at him with a strange expression. "You are not forgetting why you are here, are you Joe?" she asked.

He shook his head and backed away from her. "No. I remember your instructions mother. I told you on the phone it was going to take time. You just have to be patient."

She gave him a smile in response to his words. "Yes, I know. However, it is hard to be patient. I am staying in that seedy motel on the edge of town with nothing to do all day but think about our plan. You are living in luxury while I do not have money for a hamburger." Joe listened to his mother's complaining words. He reached in his pocket and handed her a twenty dollar bill. "This is all the cash I have. Take it and get something to eat." Maureen watched as he turned and started to walk away. "Where are you going now?" she asked him. Joe turned to his mother, "Home." Before she had a chance to respond, he had turned the corner of the alley. When she reached the sidewalk, he was no where to be seen. She took the cash and walked down the street to the small deli she had passed earlier. "That boy is getting too comfortable. I think our plan is going to have to move faster." She thought as she entered the shop.

CHAPTER TWELVE:

The walk home gave Joe time to think about the situation with his mother. He tried to understand the frustration she was feeling with Abby. He was certain that Joseph had loved his mother. He had come to realize that he would have never divorced Abby. He tried to think of a way he could convince his mother of those facts.

The life he had found with Abby and Shawn was the closest to a real family that he had ever known. They had opened their home to him without question. He knew Shawn still had some doubts about his story, but he still seemed to be willing to share his home and try to guide Joe to a better life.

When he arrived at the house, he tried to act like he had enjoyed his time in town. He told Abby that he had eaten already and after telling them good night, he retired to his loft over the garage.

Shawn sat in the den content by the fireplace. Abby voiced her concern about Joe. "Did he seem upset to you?" Shawn shook his head in response to her question. They talked for awhile and finally decided to call it a night.

When Abby joined Shawn in bed, she could not stop wondering about Joe's mood. It was not anything he said, it was just the look on his face when he walked into the house.

Shawn took her in his arms and when his passionate kisses started to arouse her, she managed to push her thoughts of Joe away. "I love you so much Abby," he said to her. As his fingers caressed her breasts and his kisses became deeper, she responded the same sentiment back to him. "My life has become so precious since you came into it," she told him.

The joining of their bodies brought complete pleasure. Abby knew her future was with Shawn. He fulfilled every desire she had both physically and mentally. She was so proud of the way he was taking Joe under his wing. She knew the boy would benefit from his guidance.

As they fell asleep in each other's arms, Abby thought about the upcoming weekend visit with Cassie and Henry. She felt apprehensive about their reaction to Joe. She had faith in her children. She hoped they would accept him into their family as she had managed to do. It might take longer for Henry, but she was confident he would warm up to Joe if he gave himself enough time.

*****

The next morning, Joe joined them in the kitchen. He took the mug of coffee from Abby and sat on the floor petting Nutmeg. "I am looking forward to getting to the shop," he told them.

Shawn smiled at his comment. "Well, I guess I did not work you hard enough yesterday. I will try to do better today." Joe laughed while he finished his coffee.

"Abby, I would like to learn more about the business end of running the antique shop if you would teach me." She told him that could be arranged. Joe inquired about where all the furniture came from that they sold in the shop. She told him about the estate sales she had traveled to recently. "Maybe I could go with you next time," he said.

"Sounds like a plan to me," she responded. "It would be fun to have some company on my next excursion." Shawn watched and listened without joining in the conversation. He was happy for Abby that Joe was showing such interest in the shop.

He knew she had wanted her children to take an interest. Since they were busy with their growing families, they had not shown any signs of interest. Not yet anyway. Maybe when they met Joe on the weekend visit, they might change their minds.

Shawn thought that Henry could very well become more interested in the shop after seeing how Joe was starting to fit in with Abby. He had tried to get closer to Henry, but it was difficult. He had such a protective nature towards Abby that he still held back when Shawn tried to start a conversation with him. Shawn felt certain that Henry would not feel comfortable knowing Joe was stepping into the role of step-son with Abby.

He did not voice any opinions to Abby about the weekend. He only intended to watch the interaction between Abby's children and Joe.

It should prove to be entertaining.

CHAPTER THIRTEEN:

The week seemed to go by fast for Abby. She was so excited to see her children. She hoped they would be open to a relationship with Joe. She knew it would take time for them to accept what Joseph had done. She was also expecting them to open their hearts to Joe.

She knew Cassie would probably be more willing to allow Joe into the family. Henry was a tougher sell. He would probably look at Joe as a threat to her security. He always seemed so protective. Even around Shawn. Abby was pleased they got along, but it would be nice if Henry could warm up more to Shawn.

She had not voiced any thoughts to either of the children about the possibility of a wedding with Shawn. They had spoken about it from time to time. Even after their recent love making, Shawn had brought up the subject.

Abby had never considered the idea of marrying again after Joseph's death. She knew the children would not be ready to accept anyone as a stepfather. After the Jonathan episode, she left that stone unturned. She decided there was no reason to stir up any problems.

Now that she had become closer to Shawn, the thoughts of marrying had become more prominent. Especially since Joe's arrival.

*****

Abby sat at the kitchen table with her coffee when Shawn came into the room. He told her good morning and got no response. When he walked over to her and leaned down for a kiss, he startled her. "Well, where were you?" he asked. Abby smiled and blushed slightly.

"Just daydreaming." She looked around to see if Joe was with him before she added. "I was thinking about a wedding." Shawn stopped pouring his coffee and turned to her. "Oh? Anyone I know?" Abby laughed at his question.

She walked over to him and kissed his lips. "Yes. A lovely couple that I have become close to. I am beginning to think they should make their partnership legal."

Before Shawn could answer, Joe came in through the kitchen door. "Hi. How is everyone today?" he asked. Shawn noticed the smile on his face. "You look happy today." Joe nodded. "Yup. I am excited about meeting my siblings. Sure, hope we can all get along. I always wanted a brother or sister. Now I will have both. Kind of neat."

Abby poured his coffee and they all sat down at the table. "Abby. Do you think they will like me?" the boy asked. "Yes, Joe. If you act like yourself, I think they will like you just fine. It might take Henry more time to warm up to the fact he has a half-brother. So don't take offense at any comments or questions he might throw at you."

Shawn looked at Joe. "Yes. He still interrogates me whenever he gets an opportunity to do so." Abby nodded and added that Henry had always been protective of her feelings after Joseph died. "He does not mean anything by his questions. He just worries about me."

The three continued their conversation through breakfast. Abby tried to reassure Joe that if he was patient, she was certain the others would find he was a happy addition to their family.

After Joe finished eating, he carried his dishes to the sink. He announced he wanted to straighten up the loft before the company arrived and left the house.

Abby stood loading the dishwasher when Shawn grabbed her from behind. She turned and he kissed her tenderly. "Now, back to our conversation." He said.

Just as Abby started to answer, they heard a car horn. She looked out the window and saw Jake's car pulling into the drive. She hugged Shawn before she grabbed her coat to run and greet her daughter. "We can pick up later when we have some time," she said as she opened the kitchen door.

Shawn smiled and nodded. "I think I will have some shopping in town later today," he thought to himself.

Before he could get outside, Cassie came rushing in the door. She waved and yelled hello as she ran past him. "Sorry Shawn. This baby has been pushing on my bladder for the past half hour. Be back in a few minutes."

Shawn stood in the kitchen laughing as he watched her waddle past him. He knew how excited Cassie and Jake were about this new baby. Even though they had little Mary who turned a year old recently, they were both so happy about welcoming a new addition to their family.

Shawn felt so close to Abby's children and their families. They were the closest that he would ever come to his own children. Even Henry with his constant questions made Shawn pleased to have him in his life. He felt they shared one common thing. Their love for Abby.

He thought about possibly marrying Abby and making them a real family. He had wanted to make her his wife from the first moment he kissed her. Now that she was thinking the same way, it was hard to keep from smiling.

"Well, hello again," Cassie said as she put her arms around him. "Sorry about earlier. Mother Nature waits for no one when you are pregnant." Shawn laughed as he returned her hug.

"You look great Cassie. This pregnancy really is showing early. Any news about the sex of your new little package?" She smiled at him and looked around behind her. "Yes, this one is a boy. Please do not tell Mom or anyone. Jake does not even know yet. He will be so thrilled to hear he is having a son."

Shawn hugged her again and promised to keep her secret. They looked up as Abby came in through the door carrying baby Mary. She walked over and handed the baby to Shawn. "Here Grandpa. She is becoming quite an armful."

The baby looked up at Shawn and squealed. He could not control his laughter. "I guess she swoons over you just like all the women," Abby told him. "Sorry ladies. Just cannot control my charm. It does affect all the women. Even the really young ones, obviously."

They stood laughing as Jake walked into the room. "What is so funny?" he asked. Cassie shook her head. "We are just seeing the effect that Shawn has on the baby. Hope it works for this one too." She answered while holding her growing stomach.

Jake leaned down and planted a kiss on his wife's stomach. "We shall see when he or she gets here." Abby put her arms out to embrace her daughter. "You look wonderful sweetie. The second time seems to agree with you much better." She told Cassie.

They all walked into the den. The baby spotted Nutmeg laying in his bed and tried to crawl over to the cat. It was more of a belly roll than a crawl, but she ended up next to Nutmeg. The cat gave the baby's hand a large lick and made no move to run away. Little Mary started to giggle so hard that she rolled over on the rug. This brought everyone else to tears with their laughter.

Abby looked around at her family and could not express the love she felt in her heart. She had a private wish that this new baby could be a son for her daughter and son-in-law. She remembered the joy she felt when she gave birth to Cassie and Henry.

The group sat in the den while Abby served everyone drinks. "Have you heard from Henry?" Cassie asked. It seemed that Abby had only answered that she had not when they heard a car pull into the driveway.

Jake looked out the window and announced Henry and family had just arrived. Abby and Shawn went to open the front door as little Hank ran up on the porch. "Nana." He yelled as he jumped into Abby's waiting arms.

Shawn reached down to keep Abby from being knocked over by her grandson's actions. "Hank. Be careful of Nana." Alice said as she joined them on the porch. Abby shook her head and just hugged Hank tighter. "He is just fine dear. I was prepared for the attack."

Henry walked up the steps and shook Shawn's outstretched hand. "Good to see you, Shawn." He helped his mother up and pulled her in for a large hug. "Mom. How are you? You look great." She gave her son a kiss on the cheek, and they entered the house arm in arm.

"I am just fine. You all are looking wonderful. She turned around and was surprised to see Annie walking alongside Henry. "Annie. You are walking so good. What a surprise."

Henry beamed at his daughter. "Yes, we thought it would be a nice surprise for you. She actually only started last week. So far, she seems to be even faster than Hank was when he started to walk."

Alice smiled at her husband. "You should be used to girls being so much more advanced than boys, my love." He rolled his eyes at his wife's comment. She poked him in the ribs and followed him inside.

Cassie and Jake met them in the hall. They retreated to the kitchen after all the hugs and kisses were completed. "What can I get you all to drink?" Abby asked. Hank shouted, "hot chocolate." She looked down at him and after lifting him onto the stool near the kitchen island, she showed him the pan of milk already heating on the stove. "Your wish is my command, young sir." She answered.

Henry looked at his sister. "Wow, sis. You are getting huge already." She punched him, "Thanks little brother. Leave it to you to turn a woman's head with compliments." Jake came to his wife's defense. "Yes, she is even more beautiful this time around." Cassie kissed her husband and thanked him for his kind words.

Everyone carried their drinks into the den. Shawn followed carrying the mug of hot chocolate for Hank. Abby brought in a platter of appetizers that she had prepared.

*****

Joe had seen the cars as they pulled into the driveway. He watched Abby and Shawn as they greeted the visiting family. He was surprised at the nervous feeling in his stomach. What if his newly found siblings rejected him. How would Abby feel about his living in the loft after her children turned down any chance of friendship with him.

He considered sneaking away and leaving before anyone caught sight of him. Then he thought about facing Maureen. She would not be pleased with that decision.

CHAPTER FOURTEEN:

Shawn walked into the kitchen to refill his coffee when he spotted Joe coming down the stairs from the loft apartment. He watched the boy wondering if he was leaving. Joe stopped when he reached the drive. He stood for a few minutes and then turned to walk over to the kitchen door.

Shawn startled Joe when he opened the door for him. The boy looked up and Shawn could see the look of fear in his eyes. "Hey Joe. No need to be worried. Cassie and Henry are both nice people. The meeting will be awkward, but it is going to be just fine." He put his arm around Joe's shoulders and gave him a small hug.

Everyone stopped talking and looked up when Shawn and Joe walked into the room. Abby smiled and walked over to stand by Joe's side. He gave her a little smile and she knew how nervous he must be feeling. She grabbed his hand and held it as she led him into the den.

Abby looked around at her children. "Well, everyone. I would like you all to meet someone. This young man is Joseph, Joe for short." Henry stood and walked over to the boy. "Hey. Nice to meet you, Joe." He said as he reached out a hand. Joe took his hand and gave it a strong shake. "Same here. Thanks." He said to Henry.

Abby walked over to Cassie. "Joe, this is my daughter Cassie." He leaned down and shook her hand. "Hello. Nice to meet you, Cassie. You look just like your mother. Very pretty." Cassie smiled at his comment. "Thank you, Joe. Flattery gets me every time." Her husband Jake offered his hand to Joe. "Yes, I will vouch for that." The group laughed.

Abby continued the introductions with Alice and Jake. Then the little ones. Hank stood and acted very grown by shaking Joe's hand. Then

Annie got bashful and hid behind her mother. Mary was too busy playing with Nutmeg to pay attention to anyone else.

Shawn sat down and Abby asked Joe if he would like something to drink or eat. "No, ma'am. Thank you." He sat down on the floor next to the fireplace.

Everyone was quiet as they waited for Abby to explain just exactly who Joe was and how he happened to be there with the family.

Abby took a deep breath and began with the explanation. "I know you are all wondering who Joe is. Let me start by telling you his entire name." She looked from Cassie to Henry. "This young man is Joseph Sampson Jr."

Cassie seemed to stop breathing for a moment. She grabbed Jake's hand. "Mother? What are you saying?" Abby continued. "I know this is going to be difficult for you to hear. It was for me too. Joe is your half-brother. Your father had an affair with Joe's mother Maureen Bishop years before he died. Joe is the result of that affair."

Henry stood and faced his mother. "How did you meet him? Did he show you proof about his parents?" Alice took his hand and tried to get him to sit down, but he refused. "How is this possible?"

Abby did not know what to say for a moment. Finally, Shawn stepped in and answered Henry's questions. "Joe had his birth certificate which he let us look at when he arrived. Your mother had photos of your father when he was a boy. There is no doubt about Joe's paternity."

Abby looked over at her daughter. Cassie sat quietly next to Jake. Tears ran down her cheeks. "Oh Cassie. Please dear try not to get upset. It is not good for the baby." Without saying a word, Cassie walked over to Joe. She knelt down by the boy and put her arms around him. "Welcome to our family Joe."

Everyone in the room watched the scene unfolding before them. Abby started to shed quiet tears when she saw her daughter's actions. Shawn took her hand. He could feel the emotion that she was trying to control finally releasing itself.

Alice leaned over and kissed her husband. She walked over to Cassie and Joe and followed the action she had seen. "Welcome Joe." He sat on the floor with the two women and his tears started to flow as well. After seeing his sister and his wife embrace the young man, Henry stood and walked over to the group now standing before him. "I do not understand how this happened exactly. I do know that you are not at fault Joe. Welcome to our family." He reached out and shook Joe's hand again. This time much stronger than earlier.

Shawn put his arm around Abby's shoulders. The scene that had unfolded in front of everyone did not need words to explain. Abby's children had in fact accepted Joe's presence. There would be further questions and much more explanation, but for now what mattered was the outpouring of love he saw.

Joe could not believe what had just happened. He stood next to his newly found family. His siblings had welcomed him into their family. He could feel the warmth and the friendship they offered him. He would never have believed this moment was possible if he had not seen it himself. How could he possibly follow his mother's plan now? He finally had a family who were ready to accept a stranger into their lives. How could she expect him to jeopardize this opportunity by placing their mother in danger? He had no idea how he would convince her to change her mind about Abby. He only knew he had to try.

CHAPTER FIFTEEN:

The rest of the afternoon went better than anyone could have planned. Abby was overtaken with pride for the way her children welcomed Joe as their sibling.

There were questions asked by both Henry and Cassie. Joe tried his best to satisfy their curiosity by answering as truthfully as he could. Shawn helped Abby prepare their dinner while the group in the den continued to get acquainted.

Abby checked on everyone to make sure they were still getting along. When she joined Shawn in the kitchen, he was relieved to see the smile on her face. "Everyone behaving themselves?" he asked. She nodded and went back to her food preparation.

"I am amazed at how well they are accepting this news. Especially Henry. I expect he will probably have some private questions for me when he gets the chance. But for now, he is being the son I knew was possible." Shawn leaned in and gave her a quick peck on the cheek.

"I have to admit. When Joe first arrived and you introduced him, I did hold my breath. I waited for an explosion, but I was so pleased too with the response. Henry and Cassie are definitely following your example. They are really something."

She nodded and could not speak because of the catch in her throat. Shawn saw her face. "No crying in the salad please." He told her. They both were laughing when Cassie walked into the kitchen.

"Can I do anything?" she asked. "No. I think we have everything under control. How is the reunion going?" Abby asked her daughter. "Well, mom. I have to say this is not what we were expecting when you asked us to visit. I had no idea that Dad would ever have an affair. I am sorry that you had to find out this way. I do agree with Henry. Whatever Dad did was not Joe's fault. There is no reason we should be resentful toward him."

Abby smiled and walked around to her daughter. She hugged her tightly. "I am so proud of you both. This day could have turned out so different. I hoped you could open your heart to Joe as we have. He is a remarkable young man." Shawn nodded in agreement. "Your mother is certainly correct in that observation. He pitched in and did a great job on the loft over the garage. I was really surprised how pleased he was with the living arrangement we offered. It is not the greatest, but he said it was much better than what he had been used to recently."

Abby continued, "Shawn is right. He seems so thankful for every little gesture. I get the feeling he did not have too good a relationship with his mother before she passed away. He has even been an asset to us in the shop. Whatever job we give him, he gives us one hundred percent participation. He actually has some really good skills with the paintbrush."

Cassie sat at the island listening to them. "He does seems sincere about his feelings for you both." She looked over at Shawn, "He even seems to understand why you did not trust him when he first arrived. He said the one common area between you both is the way you both care about mom." Shawn laughed. "Yes, I guess I did give him a bad time at first." He grabbed Abby for a hug, "I have to protect my lady."

Cassie smiled and gave him a quick kiss on her way out of the room. Abby looked at him, "your lady, huh?" Shawn kissed her quickly before the kids saw them. "Yes. And as soon as I get the approval of your children, I plan to propose and make it official."

Abby almost dropped the casserole she was lifting from the oven when she heard Shawn's comment. "You are not going to ask their permission. Are you serious?" He took the hot pan from her and placed it on the island before she lost control.

"I certainly am. I want to start out on the right foot as their step-father. There is to be no hidden agenda on either side. I want them to know just how much I love you and I need them to air any of the issues they may have with me entering the family."

Abby looked around to make sure she had not forgotten anything before she announced dinner was ready. "Can we get through our first meal together without getting into any talk of a marriage?"

She did not see Henry walking in the room behind her. When he overheard her comment, he looked at Shawn. Before Abby saw him, he came up behind her and gave her a hug. Startled, she started to explain what she meant. Henry stopped her.

"Mom, I will pretend I did not hear your words so Cassie can be surprised." Looking at Shawn, he said, "I am happy for the both of you. Shawn has shown how he cares about you. If he is willing to take on this crazy group as his own, then I will not stand in his way."

Abby kissed him on the cheek and did not say anything. He could tell by the smile on her face, how happy she was. He knew Shawn would care for her and keep her happy and safe. That was all that mattered to him.

Henry walked into the hall and announced to everyone that dinner was ready. He winked at Shawn as he went to help Alice with the children.

Shawn just stood completely amazed at what had just happened.

CHAPTER SIXTEEN:

Everyone walked into the dining room after hearing Henry's announcement. Cassie and Alice helped carry in the food while Henry and Jake got the kids settled in their highchairs. Hank took Joe by the hand and led him over to the table. "Uncle Joe. Sit by me." He said to the boy. Abby smiled at Joe and decided her surprise had turned out in the very best result possible.

Before everyone started eating, Shawn stood at the end of the table. "I would like to make a toast before we enjoy this wonderful meal." The group all took their glasses and waited for Shawn. "I would like to thank your mother for the food laid out before us. I also want to say how proud I am of all of you. Your mother and I were not certain of your feelings when you met Joe. However, you proved what loving and thoughtful people you are today. I think I can speak for Joe when I say thank you all for your showing of love." Joe smiled at Shawn's speech and watched as the entire family joined in with saying, "here, here."

Joe looked around the table and without standing, he said thanks to each person. Hank looked around. "Can we eat now?" They all laughed as Henry filled his son's plate. Abby looked across the table at Shawn and he winked at her. "I think this is one of the happiest days of my life," she thought to herself.

The dinner proved to be as tasty as it appeared. There was laughter and chatting during the meal. Joe thought how relaxed he felt amid his new family. They had all welcomed him sincerely. He laughed as he watched the toddlers enjoy their food while making a complete mess. There were no harsh words. Their parents cleaned up the food that did not make it into their mouths.

Abby had put towels around their necks, so they were able to keep their clothes clean. Nutmeg walked around under the table, stopping to eat a tasty bit of meat or anything that appealed to him.

Mary started giggling when she saw the cat searching for a snack. "Kitty, kitty." Abby walked over to her granddaughter and planted a big kiss on her messy cheek. "Yes, Nutmeg is our resident floor cleaner."

Henry added, "You really need a dog mom. They make better floor cleaners. Not as fussy as a cat." Abby nodded in agreement. "Yes, you are probably correct Henry. However, we have a houseful enough without adding a dog. Besides, I do not think Nutmeg would be too pleased to share his warm bed or our attention."

After everyone had finished, Cassie and Alice told Abby to sit and rest while they cleared the table. As they started to fill the dishwasher, Shawn appeared in the doorway. "I have to run out for a short time." Abby looked at him curiously. He saw the question she was about to ask. "Nothing to worry about. Just something that must be picked up at the store. I won't be long."

He blew her a kiss and rushed out the front door. Cassie and Alice looked at each other but said nothing. Abby walked into the den and found Joe on the floor with Hank and Mary playing Candyland. "Oh, I see you found the games," she said to them.

Hank looked up and smiled. "I am ahead Grandma. Look, Uncle Joe is way down at the beginning." Everyone laughed and Abby walked back into the kitchen. Just as she walked in Alice was leaning toward Cassie and stopped talking when she saw Abby in the doorway.

"All right you two. What is going on? Am I missing something?" The two women looked at each other and just smiled. Cassie answered her mother. "Of course not mom. We were just gossiping. Nothing important." She looked at both of their faces and did not accept Cassie's explanation for one minute. Deciding to not ask any further questions, she started to put away the leftovers in the refrigerator.

When they had finished in the kitchen, they all joined the men in the other room. The game had been completed and Joe was sitting on the floor reading a book to the little ones. Baby Annie had fallen asleep on her father's lap. It almost looked like Henry was ready to join her.

Abby stood in the doorway and smiled at her family. How proud she was at this very moment. She had no idea what life had in store for her in the future. All she wanted to concentrate on was this time in her life. She was surrounded by her loving children and grandchildren. She had a man who loved her. There was no possible way that life could get any better.

*****

Shawn drove into town and parked in front of the jewelry store. When he entered the clerk looked up from his work. "Hello Shawn. I was pleased to get your call earlier. We have everything ready as you asked."

Shawn examined the box the clerk handed him. Everything was exactly as he had said. "She is going to be very happy. You did a great job." After he paid the clerk, he walked back to his car.

As he backed out of the parking space and drove down the street, he did not take any notice to the woman who watched from across the street.

Maureen recognized the man from the antique shop. She knew from her son's description that he was Abby's boyfriend. Curious as to what he had just bought, Maureen crossed the street. When she entered the jewelry store, the clerk greeted her. "Good afternoon. May I help you with something today?" Maureen said she was just browsing.

After minutes, she addressed the clerk. "I just saw my friend's boyfriend leave the store. I bet he was buying her a birthday gift." The clerk smiled and answered. "I do not think so. Unless he is proposing to her on her birthday."

She looked at the man and tried to act nonchalant. "Oh, that's right. He did tell me in confidence that he was planning on asking her to marry. I did not realize he was doing it so soon."

As Maureen walked out the door, she turned to the clerk. "We must keep this a secret. Just in case he does not ask her today." The clerk nodded and said he would not say a word.

Maureen walked outside and looked around. There were only a few people on the sidewalk, but no one was giving her any attention. She managed to get to the end of the street quietly. As she entered the small park, she walked to a bench that was empty.

"Proposing, is he? Well, I will make sure there is no happy ending to that proposal." She tried to reach Joe, but he was not picking up his calls. When she heard the call go to voicemail, she hung up.

"Joe. Where are you? What is going on with your family meeting? I bet they are all mad as wet hens to hear about their father's affair. I know Joseph was leaving them for us. He just needed time to plan how he would explain his other family to Abby and her brats. Well, now they know they did not matter to him. I am the woman he truly loved and wanted to live with."

CHAPTER SEVENTEEN:

Joe glanced at his phone and noticed the missed call. He knew his mother had tried to reach him. He was certain she was probably in one of her moods. She would not be pleased when he explained how the family meeting had gone. He thought about lying and trying to downplay how Cassie and Henry had welcomed him without any hesitation.

By the end of the evening, he was not looking forward to returning her call. He had agreed to meet everyone the next morning for breakfast before they returned home. As he walked over to his loft all his thoughts were about how considerate and warm his newfound siblings had been. When Cassie first found out who he was he watched her face. She began to cry, and he was positive she would be furious about the affair. When she instead went to him and took him into her arms with a huge welcoming hug, he could not believe what was happening.

Then even more so when Henry reached out his hand as a warm welcome into the family. He laid in his bed finding it difficult to sleep. He knew he should have returned his mother's call but did not want his feeling of happiness ruined by her words of destruction. He had to figure out a way to change her mind about Abby. Maybe he could arrange a meeting and she could see for herself what a special woman Abby really was.

Then he remembered that he had told Abby and Shawn that his mother had passed away. He did not want them to find out about his lies. He felt so happy to finally have a large family that really included him. His fears of confronting them all with the truth for his appearance would certainly be the end of that happiness.

*****

Abby and Shawn sat up talking for a short time after everyone had gone upstairs. She was so excited and pleased with how the entire evening had ended. "I cannot believe how wonderful my children responded to Joe. I tried to prepare myself for the worst possible reaction to him. I do not think I have ever felt prouder of both Cassie and Henry. They have grown into such warm and caring adults."

Shawn looked at her and smiled. "How could they be anything else when they have you to set such good examples. Abby, you have raised two of the finest adults I have ever met. I was not looking forward to the meeting. I really thought Cassie would be accepting of Joe, but Henry would be a totally different story."

She nodded. "Yes, I agree with you. When he walked over to Joe and extended his hand as a sincere welcome, I had to control my urge to cry out." Shawn laughed. "That would have startled everyone." She laughed with him after agreeing with his words.

When they finally climbed the stairs, Shawn had one thing on his mind. He could feel the ring box in his pocket. Should he ask her now? He had a feeling the family would be upset if they were not present for his proposal. He placed the box in his dresser drawer while Abby was in the bathroom. "I will do it tomorrow during breakfast," he finally decided.

He looked up as she walked into the bedroom. He could not believe he was lucky enough to have found such a beautiful woman to be his partner. She amazed him every day with her ability to find the good in everyone she met. The way she had accepted Joe into their home, had at first worried him. Now after the weeks they had spent with him, he found he was as fond of the boy as she was. It had just taken him longer to accept Joe's story. Now with Cassie and Henry allowing Joe to join the family, he could not be more pleased.

He pulled the quilt back so Abby could join him in bed. As soon as she was by his side he reached for her body. She moaned when his caresses reached her most sensitive spots. "Shawn. I love you so much. I want you." She whispered.

He leaned down and kissed her passionately. As his lips moved on to her breasts, she completely lost herself. When he pulled her over to be on top of him, she was more than ready to receive him inside her. As they moved together Abby felt totally complete. He fondled her breasts as his body consumed her. He managed to bring her to heights that took her breath away. When he felt her body tighten over him, he allowed himself to join her in complete joy and satisfaction.

Afterwards, they lay in each other's arms. Exhausted but completely happy, Abby kissed his smooth chest. He did not say a word but just enjoyed their closeness. When he heard her soft breathing, he allowed himself to join her in sleep.

CHAPTER EIGHTEEN:

Joe woke the next day feeling exhausted. His short bouts of sleep were filled with his mother. She was yelling at him about Abby and her family. She threatened to confront Abby if he did not do something soon. He could still hear her voice as he opened his eyes.

When he looked around the loft, he realized he was alone. The voice of his mother was only lingering in his mind. Dragging his tired body from the bed, he looked outside. The sun was shining, and it looked like another beautiful day.

He remembered the events of the day before. The welcoming of his sister and brother and their families had filled him with hope for the future. He had always wanted to be part of a huge loving family. His mother had tried her best to provide him with what he needed. She had not succeeded and finally gave up trying after his father died.

She became consumed with hatred for Abby and her children. She used all her energy to think of ways to hurt Abby. When she finally decided to have Joe work his way in with Abby and her family, she felt that would be the solution to all her problems. The money they had would support her and Joe in the way she felt she deserved.

Joe knew she intended to not only drain Abby of her money, but she wanted total revenge. She felt that could only be achieved by killing Abby. She then planned to take over the antique shop and have all the good fortune she thought Joseph intended for her.

While he dressed for work, he tried to think about what he could say to his mother to dissuade her of her plans of destroying Abby. Before he had a chance to leave the loft his phone rang. He saw the number and knew it was his mother calling.

"Morning mom." He said. The scream he heard on the other end startled him. "Where the hell have you been? Why didn't you call me last night after your meeting with Abby and her brats?" Joe thought about hanging up for a split second. He knew if he did, she would probably show up at the shop.

"It was late by the time we went to sleep. Sorry. I did not want to disturb you. I figured we would talk today." He waited for a response and after what seemed like an hour, his mother finally calmed down long enough to speak. "I waited up until midnight for your call. How did those people react to your presence?"

He hesitated and started to lie, when he thought it was the time for truth instead. "Well mom. The reaction to my being part of their family went better than anyone expected. They welcomed me literally with open arms. There were hugs and tears all around. It was great. Cassie and Henry turned out to be just like their mother Abby. They all acted like the fault was with their father and I did not deserve any of their anger or blame for the situation."

Maureen heard her son's words. Her fury boiled to the surface. "What? You mean they treated you in a good way? How could they blame your father? The fault lies with their mother. She was never enough woman to keep your father satisfied."

Joe listened and refused to let the situation get worse. "Mom. I know this is not what you were hoping for, and I am sorry for you. But I am very happy for me. I finally found the family I always wanted. People that would accept me and truly care about me. They showed me more love in hours than I have felt for years. You must forget about your plan for revenge and just move on with your life. I have found the place I want to call home now."

Joe waited for his mother to respond. Instead, all he heard was a click on the other end of the call. He stood with the phone in his hand. He looked up when he heard a soft knock on the door. For a moment he expected to see Maureen when he looked out the window. Instead, he saw Abby smiling at him.

"Hi." He said as he opened the door. He laughed when he looked down and saw Hank standing next to his grandmother. "Well, hi there Hank. How are you today?" he asked as he knelt by the boy.

"Hi Uncle Joe. I came over with grandma to ask if you are ready for breakfast." Joe nodded and took the little boy's hand as he helped him down the steps. "Grandma made pancakes and sausage. It looks yummy." Joe laughed as Hank pulled him across the driveway to the kitchen door.

Abby watched them and told Joe that Hank refused to eat until he was at the table. "Really? Well, little man. We can dive into those pancakes together." Hank laughed and ran inside the house ahead of them. "I found Uncle Joe. We are going to dive into them pancakes," he announced as he ran into the dining room.

Everyone greeted Joe. "We have all been waiting for you Joe. Hank told us we could not begin until you were in your chair." Henry helped Hank into his chair. "Sit by me Uncle Joe," the little boy yelled. Abby leaned by Joe and told him, "You have made quite a hit with our little guy." He nodded and sat down.

"OK, I think we are all present and accounted for now. Please dig in before the food gets any colder," Shawn told the group. "Joe, good to see you this morning." He added. "Thanks Shawn. There is no place I would rather be right at this moment," Joe responded.

*****

Maureen sat in her motel room trying to understand what she had just heard from her son. How could he have talked to her that way. She had raised him by herself for so many years. She knew she was not the greatest of mothers, but she had tried. It was all that woman's fault. She had filled his head with crazy ideas. She did not really care about him. She had probably told her brats to pretend to welcome him into their family. They were just playing with his mind. "They are just worried he wants their money. I bet that woman already has plans in place to get him out of the way."

Joseph had always acted so affectionate with her whenever he would visit. When she told him about being pregnant, he had been quiet. He explained later how his plans would have to change with a baby on the way. He said it would be harder to leave Abby and his children. He told Maureen that he would lose everything if he filed for divorce. Of course, she had no reason to think he was lying to her.

There was no way he would not choose her over Abby. She was prettier and had a much better shape. She had seen Abby and thought she was so plain looking. There was no flare with her makeup or the way she dressed. Joseph always commented about how pretty she looked when he would take her to bed.

There were times he wanted to try something new that seemed slightly strange to Maureen. She always agreed with his demands. She loved him and was ready to go along with anything just to keep him interested. She never got the impression he was using her sexually. She did get satisfaction from their love making. Granted he was more interested in his own pleasure. His gratification came first. But wasn't that the way all men acted. At least all that she had ever been with.

CHAPTER NINETEEN:

Breakfast lasted quite some time. Joe was concerned about getting to work late. Then Shawn and Abby reminded him they were the owners and allowed to open the shop whenever they decided.

Hank took Joe outside to play after they finished eating. Mary toddled along with him, and Joe kept a watchful eye on both the children. Henry watched from the kitchen window as the children ran around chasing Joe through the piles of leaves.

"I must admit. I am impressed with that young man. When I first heard who he was, I felt angry. Then I saw Cassie's reaction and realized it was our father who had been at fault not Joe. Even though we did not see father all that much, we still had more of his attention through the years than Joe had."

Abby smiled at her son's words. "I am very proud of you son. You and Cassie have shown what caring people you are. We were concerned about what your response would be when you met Joe. We were apprehensive at first too. But after we got better acquainted with him, we saw the good person underneath. He did have a rough life growing up, but this is his chance to see what life can be with a big family."

She hugged her son and walked over to join Cassie and Alice who were clearing the dishes. "You cooked Mom. Just sit and keep us company." Cassie told her. "Yes, I cooked. But you are pregnant. I do have to say how beautiful you look this time. Maybe that means this little one is a boy."

Cassie glanced at Alice and then turned to Abby. "Well actually mom, I have not told Jake yet. We are having twins this time and they are, in fact, both boys." Alice turned to watch Abby's reaction to Cassie's statement. "What? Twins? Oh, my goodness." She sat for minutes while she thought about her daughter's explanation. "When are you going to let Jake know? He is going to be so excited."

Cassie agreed with Abby. "Yes, he is going to be thrilled. I am having an ultrasound next week and the doctor has agreed to keep the secret until Jake can see for himself." Abby looked at Alice. "You knew about this?" Alice nodded. "Yes, I thought Cassie looked so much larger this time. When I commented last night, she whispered the truth to me. I did not even say anything to Henry. He does have trouble with secrets sometimes." The women all laughed.

Shawn walked into the room and looked at the group. "What is so amusing out here ladies?" Abby just shook her head. "Nothing dear. Just a joke for women's ears." He smiled at her. "Well, if you are all done with the dishes your presence is required in the den." He said to them as he opened the door and called Joe and the children inside.

Everyone filed into the den and Henry moved to make room for his wife in the chair. Joe and the kids rushed into the room. When Abby and the women were all seated, Shawn stood in the doorway. Looking around the room at everyone he took a deep breath and walked in towards Abby. She looked at his face which appeared to be very serious. "Shawn? Is something wrong?" she asked.

He leaned towards her and placed a kiss on her cheek. He stood and began his speech, "No my love. Everything is just perfect. I am looking around this room and see a large family of loving people. I must admit that I did not think I would ever have children or grandchildren. Abby, you have given me both. I could not be more blessed. I love you all so very much. I thank you all for accepting me into your lives. The only way my life could get any better would be for you to answer my questions," he knelt in front of Abby and reached into his pocket.

When she saw the ring box he held, she gasped. Unable to find her voice she looked at Shawn's face. "Abby, would you do me the honor of accepting this ring and becoming my wife?"

Abby felt the tears that started down her cheeks. She glanced at her children. There was no sound in the room. Even the babies were quiet. "Shawn. I am speechless." She answered. He looked at her face and for a moment thought he was going to hear an answer of no to his proposal. Finally, she smiled, "Yes, I would love to marry you."

He stood and pulled her into his arms as the entire family clapped and cheered. Cassie and Alice cried. Henry reached for Shawn's hand. Jake did the same after he handed his wife a tissue. Joe looked around and joined in the celebration. The children all laughed and yelled even though they really did not understand why.

Abby was still in Shawn's arms as the family surrounded them. She looked at him and Cassie heard her mother's words. "I love you so much Shawn." Shawn told Abby how he loved her. "I even spoke to Henry last night and got his permission." She laughed as she looked at her son. Henry gave a shrug "He was very persuasive mom. I could not say no."

They all laughed and when the group finally got control and sat down, Alice appeared in the doorway with a tray of drinks to celebrate the news. "Champagne for most of us and sparkling cider for Cassie and the children," she said.

They sat drinking and laughing. Abby could not believe what had happened. She looked at the beautiful ring on her hand. "I wanted to ask you last night but decided to wait until this morning. I thought you might want your family to be present," Abby looked him, "You mean our family."

CHAPTER TWENTY:

Everyone decided it was time for them to leave. After all the hugs and goodbyes, Abby and Shawn stood on the front porch with Joe and waved to the family as they drove away.

Joe saw the tears in Abby's eyes. "That was a great visit. I really like your family, Abby. Thanks for making me feel like one of them." Joe said as he turned to go back into the house.

Shawn stood on the porch holding Abby. He knew how she would miss her children, so he just held her until she calmed down. When she heard Joe's comments, she felt the tears flowing again. He had become so special to her and Shawn in the short time they spent together. She felt relieved that Cassie and Henry had opened their hearts to him as well.

Looking up at Shawn, Abby smiled through her tears. "Do you feel like opening the shop today?" he asked. Abby nodded. "Yes, I think that is just what I need." They walked inside to find Joe. He was in the den sitting with Nutmeg on his lap. "See? Even Nutmeg has accepted you into our family." Shawn told him.

Joe laughed and asked if they were going to open the shop. "Yes. We were just coming to find you. Are you ready for another hard day at work?" Abby said to him. Joe stood up and said he was ready and willing to do whatever jobs she had in mind.

Shawn grabbed Abby for a hug. "I am certain she will come up with some ideas for both of us before we reach the front door." They both laughed and Joe followed them outside to the car.

*****

Maureen sat in her small motel room trying to gather her thoughts. She had decided after talking to her son that she needed to go ahead with her plan to eliminate Abby. She knew she would have to find a way for the shop to be turned over to her and Joe. Once she was able to acquire the shop and have all of Abby's other assets changed to her son's name she could follow through with her promise to Joseph.

She knew he would have wanted them to be secure in their future. The other children he had would all be provided for through their own resources. She was the one that mattered, not Abby. She was the one who had loved Joseph and given in to his every request in bed. Now was the time in her life that she deserved to be comfortable and secure in her finances.

She had held down various jobs while Joe was a child. None of them paid very well and all her paychecks were used to buy food and keep a roof over his head. She had managed to survive on her own after Joseph's death. She was now a woman in her fifties and still attractive. She knew with the proper clothes and makeup she would be able to find another man who would love her.

Maureen knew Joe was upset with her and voiced his enthusiasm on the phone about his new family. She would make sure they did not think fondly of him before her plan was completed. When they heard about his deception to gain Abby's trust and take their inheritance for himself, she knew they would not feel so open to their new half-brother.

She looked in the small vanity mirror at her reflection. With her dark glasses and sun hat, she knew no one would have any idea what her real identity was. She had checked into the motel with an alias so there was no reason anyone should question her presence in Cobble Bay.

CHAPTER TWENTY-ONE:

The ride into town was spent with conversation and laughter. Shawn was teasing Uncle Joe about the immediate affection little Hank had shown him. "That little guy took a liking to you almost at first sight." Joe agreed with him as he smiled about the boy's calling him Uncle Joe. "He is really a smart little boy. He could tell right away just how special his new uncle was," said Abby.

Joe blushed by their kind words. "I think he was the special one," said Joe. "In fact, the entire family were great. I think I am going to like having older siblings. It is a whole new experience for me. All the years I was growing up, I wished for a bigger family."

Abby turned to look at Joe. "Your mother never dated anyone else after Joseph passed?" He shook his head in response. "She always said he was the love of her life. He was always good to us, but it would have been nice to see her find someone else to care for her."

Abby glanced over at Shawn and decided to leave the subject alone. At least for now anyway.

*****

Maureen had stopped at the café across from the antique shop. She did not see anyone around and wondered if it would be open later. She sat at a booth in the back where she could watch the shop from a nearby window. She only had five dollars, so she just ordered coffee and a muffin.

As she sat watching, she was pleased to see the car pull up in front of the shop. When Joe got out of the back seat, she could see the smile on his face. He seemed so happy with Abby and her man. "That will change soon," she thought. She continued to watch the three enter the shop. When she finished her coffee, she paid and walked outside. "I think I will walk past and see if Joe is near to the front." As she crossed the street, she looked in the front display windows, but there was no movement inside the shop. The CLOSED sign still hung in the door.

Not wanting to be noticed, she walked down the street acting like the other tourists she saw strolling on the sidewalk. She passed the other shops and smiled at the people she saw. When she got to the park, she found a bench in the shade and sat down. "I have to plan how to get that woman out of our lives for good. If it could look like an accident, maybe I could get friendly with her man. He is nice to look at and he already likes Joe. That could work out for both of us."

She sat consumed by her thoughts for an hour or so. Finally, she decided to walk back to the motel. As she walked past the shop again, she almost ran into Shawn and Abby as they walked out the front door. "Oh, sorry. Guess I need to watch where I am walking." She said to them.

Smiling back at her, Abby told her they needed to be more aware of people on the sidewalk too. After telling Maureen to have a nice day, they continued across the street to the café.

Maureen did not see Joe watching from the doorway. She hurried down the street and turned the corner before he walked out of the shop. He watched her rushing around to the alleyway. "Oh boy. Just what are you up to mom?" he thought to himself.

He heard Shawn call to him and when he looked up, he saw them wave as they entered the café. He hurried across the street to join them before his mother saw him.

CHAPTER TWENTY-TWO:

Joe spotted Shawn and Abby in a booth by the window. He walked over to join them. His thoughts were on his mother, and he tried hard not to show his concern. "Hey you two. Sorry I was so slow. Just checking the door to make sure it was secure."

Shawn smiled and handed him a menu. "You are acting very mature Joe. That is good to see." Joe nodded and tried to concentrate on the menu. He found it hard to focus on anything except wondering about his mother. He had no idea what her next move might be. As he stared at the menu in front of him, his mind was elsewhere.

He looked up when Shawn poked him. The waitress was standing nearby waiting for his order. Abby and Shawn were looking at him. "Is everything all right?" Abby asked. Joe nodded. "Yes, ma'am. I got lost in thought for a minute. Sorry to hold you all up from ordering lunch."

He gave the waitress his order and took a big gulp from his water glass. "What is up with you today?" Shawn asked him. "You are not usually in the clouds." Joe hung his head and tried to think of a legitimate explanation for his behavior.

"I guess I am still thinking about the weekend. I was very surprised with the way Cassie and Henry accepted me into the family. They did not even hesitate for a minute. I was afraid they would think I was not being honest." He looked at Abby. "I am so thankful to you Abby for the way you have opened your home and your heart to me. It is a totally new experience. I guess it is hard to believe all this is really happening. Everything I have thought about since I was a kid is finally coming true."

Abby could see the honesty on Joe's face. She wanted to grab him and hug him but knew it would be embarrassing to him in the café. "Joe. I hope you realize by now that Shawn and I both think highly of you. We know you would never do anything to cause problems with us or the family. You just have to accept what we offer and enjoy this new life. We want only the best for you."

Joe heard her words. It was hard to keep his emotions under control. All he could think about was Maureen and what her next move would be. He knew he had to face her before anything happened further.

Their lunch came and everyone ate quietly. Shawn watched Joe and for no clear reason he had a feeling of something bad. He decided not to mention it to Abby, but he intended to speak to Joe alone. It just seemed the boy had some deeper problems than he was not admitting to either of them. He hoped he could get Joe to open up to him, man to man.

As they walked outside heading back to the shop, Joe asked Abby if she minded if he left early. "I promise to make up the time tomorrow. I just remembered there was something I really need to take care of today." She told him it was fine, and he did not have to concern himself about making up the time. "You have been working so hard in the shop there really is not much else that needs to be done."

When they went inside Joe glanced back to make sure he did not spot Maureen on the street. After feeling relieved that she was not around, he walked over to the attic door. He had wanted to get upstairs and straighten up the area as a surprise to Shawn.

Shawn had followed Abby into the office and neither of them saw Joe as he slipped through the door to the upstairs. He found the light switch and looked up the stairs. When he noticed light showing under the upstairs door, he became curious. Maybe someone left the light on by mistake, he thought.

When he opened the upstairs door, he looked around the room. He realized the light was from the large window at the end of the space. Looking around he noticed the old trunks pushed into the corner. There were old dressers and file cabinets on the opposite wall. The space did not look in too bad a shape. He took the broom that he had brought and started sweeping the floor.

Before he got too far, he noticed a cold draft. Not sure where it came from, he looked around the room. There did not seem to be any large cracks in the roof that would let in cold air. As he started to walk closer to the window, the door opened, and Shawn stood looking at him. "What are you doing?" he asked the boy.

Joe jumped when he heard Shawn's voice. "I wanted to surprise you by cleaning the attic. It is not in as bad a shape as I expected. I felt a draft and was trying to find where it came from."

Shawn walked over to Joe. "We heard you from downstairs. You did not have to bother yourself with the attic. We try to sweep the cobwebs every now and then. Otherwise, it is empty and not something you need to concern yourself with."

He took the broom from Joe and motioned him toward the door. Shawn glanced behind him as he closed the door. There was nothing to see. No ghostly figures appeared which made him sign in relief.

When they got back down the stairs, Abby walked over to them. She looked at Shawn and he winked and nodded to her. "Everything ship shape upstairs?" she asked when she saw the broom in Shawn's hand.

"Yup. Everything is just fine Captain." Uttered Shawn with a salute. She laughed along with Joe. "Glad to hear the ship is still afloat," she replied. Just as she was going to ask further, the door opened, and a customer entered the shop.

Shawn gestured toward the woman who walked inside. "You boys get back to your duties and the captain will oversee this sale." They looked at each other and walked into the back room.

Abby greeted the woman as she entered the shop and asked if she needed any help. Joe followed Shawn into the back. He looked over his shoulder to make sure the customer did not turn out to be Maureen. When he was satisfied with the stranger he saw, he caught up to Shawn.

"What do you need today?" Joe asked Shawn. Shawn explained he wanted Joe to wash the front display windows inside and out. He thought about trying to talk to Joe about his mood but thought it would be better done at home.

Joe took the cleaning supplies he needed and walked out to the front windows. He decided to tackle the outside first and carried the bucket and squeegee out the front door. As he worked, he kept looking up and down the sidewalk for Maureen. He knew she was probably watching from an alley.

*****

Maureen saw Joe as he walked out of the shop. She stood in the shadows across the street and watched him as he washed the large window. She saw him glance around every now and then. "Probably looking for me," she thought.

She finally decided to walk across the street to the shop. She would act very nonchalant and in case anyone saw her she would pretend to be asking Joe about the shops nearby.

Joe turned just as Maureen reached his side. He looked inside quickly and saw that Abby had her back turned toward the window. He did not see Shawn and assumed he was in the office.

"What are you doing here?" he asked his mother. "Are you trying to get noticed?" Maureen smiled at him. "Just stopped to say hello to my hard-working son. I was waiting for a call, and you disappointed me again. We need to talk about our plans."

Joe listened and told her that he was leaving work early. "I will meet you at the motel later. We can discuss things then." She nodded and walked down the street pretending to follow his directions.

Joe went back to the window and cleaned the same area several times before he finally controlled his anger. He moved over to the adjacent window and after washing it he moved inside to finish the job.

Shawn had been watching Joe when he talked to the woman outside. She seemed pleasant, but he could see Joe's face getting red. He knew the boy was angry. He did not understand why, but fully intended to find out when he confronted him later at home.

CHAPTER TWENTY-THREE:

Joe finished with the windows. He brought his supplies into the back room. Shawn was fixing another cup of coffee. "How about taking a break?" he asked Joe.

"Thanks, but I was just getting ready to leave. Abby said it was all right to leave early. I will see you later at the house," he replied as he walked out the back door.

Abby was in the office when Shawn walked in with a cup of coffee for her. "Join me in a cup?" he asked as he sat down in front of her desk. Smiling she took the cup and thanked him. "You knew Joe was leaving early?" he asked. Abby nodded. "Yes, he had errands to take care of. Why do you ask?"

"No reason. Did you happen to see the woman he was talking to outside?" Abby shook her head no as she drank her coffee. "Anyone we know?" Shawn told her he did not recognize the woman. "The conversation was short, but it looked like it bothered Joe. He had a strange look when he came back inside."

"What did you think when you heard the sounds up in the attic earlier?" she asked. Shawn looked over at her. "I thought for a moment our earlier houseguests had returned. When I went upstairs, he was sweeping so I did not say anything to make him ask any questions. I think we have had our fill of ghostly appearances."

Abby agreed. "Are you going to ask him any questions when we get home about the woman you saw?" she asked him. Shawn thought for a moment, "I have not decided. Maybe I will just wait and see if I see her again. Might just be someone from his past who he was not happy to see again." She nodded and they sat quietly enjoying their coffee before the next group of customers.

*****

Joe walked to the park after he left the shop. He expected to see Maureen waiting for him, but she was not to be found. "Guess she must be at the motel." He was relieved that they would not have to be seen together.

When he got to her room, he knocked and then tried the doorknob. Walking inside he found her sitting in the small chair by the window. "I saw you walking up in the parking lot," she commented. "How did you manage to get away early? No problems with your new bosses?"

He could tell by her tone that she had gotten herself in a mood again. It would not be easy trying to talk her into backing away from Abby, but he decided he had no choice but to try.

"They did not say anything when I asked for the afternoon off. I know you do not want to hear it, but they have treated me with nothing but kindness since I first arrived on their doorstep." Joe waited for Maureen to get angry. Instead, she seemed to be calming down from her previous show of anger.

"You know they are just pretending to care about you. I hope you are not falling for their false showing of love for you. How could that woman possibly care for the bastard son of her husband? She must be devastated to think he had an affair and fell in love with another woman. How could she possibly accept you in her family? That would be a constant reminder of her husband's betrayal to their marriage."

Joe listened and tried to explain what a kind and loving person Abby was. He told her of all the things she had done for him. He told her how Shawn had mistrusted him at first, but finally came around. He also explained in detail about the weekend meeting with her children.

"Her little grandson Hank even started calling me Uncle Joe. I thought that was pretty special."

He waited for her to say something. Instead, she just listened with a strange smile on her face. "That is wonderful to hear. They will have no problem turning against you when they learn the truth. That way their mother will get angry at them for treating you badly and drop them from her will. This might be the best thing that could happen to bring our plan together.

Joe could not believe what she was saying. What made her think that Abby would ever turn against her own children to stand up for him. "She will be just as upset with me if she found out how I have lied and deceived them all."

Maureen thought for a moment. "Not if she thinks you were only doing what your mother asked of you on her death bed. If she is as caring about you as you think that could work to our advantage. Those brats would certainly be worried about you making a claim on her money. The more they push against you, the more she will support you. Even her man will go along with her thinking. He seems devoted to her and will agree with whatever she wants to do."

Joe realized he was not going to talk Maureen out of her original plan. "How are you planning to get control of her money? I cannot believe you are seriously considering killing Abby."

She did not comment. The smile that appeared on her face told Joe that was exactly what she had in mind.

CHAPTER TWENTY-FOUR:

Joe tried for hours to convince his mother to stop her crazy plan. When he finally realized he was not making any progress he walked out of the motel room.

Maureen still sat in the same chair near the window. She watched as Joe walked out of the parking lot. She thought about his words. For a fleeting moment she considered what he had pleaded. Maybe she could live without the responsibility of caring for Joe. He was earning money for himself. She could move away and start a new life. Find a job and a small apartment.

The more she thought, the more upset she became. He was her son. Joseph's gift to her. She would not leave him to another woman. Joseph had loved her more than Abby. He had told her many times about how happy she made him. He felt fulfilled with their lovemaking. She knew their sex had been more for him, but she accepted that. He was the man and as his woman her job was to please his every desire regardless of her own feelings.

She had learned that from her mother. She had watched her parents as a child. Her mother did everything her husband demanded of her. She raised Maureen as her husband dictated. Everything he wanted was given by her mother.

She started to think about the years she had become a teenager. Her father had started to treat her differently. He looked at her in a strange way when they were sitting watching television at night. When he came into her room the first night, she felt happy to see him. As he sat down on her bed, he spoke softly to her. He told her what a beautiful girl she was and how he loved her.

All the while he spoke, he started touching her young body. She tried not to be afraid. This was her father. He loved her. He would never do anything to hurt her.

When his hands became more intimate with her body, she found the fear harder to push away. She did not speak or pull away. When he finished his physical abuse of her body, he warned her not to say anything about what he had done. "It would make your mother upset to think you were a bad girl."

He would kiss her on the forehead and leave her bedroom. She would curl up in a ball under the covers trying to make herself as small as possible. She did not understand what had just been done to her. That was the beginning of years to follow.

Her friends and classmates did not understand why she became so quiet with them. She did not talk in class and her teachers became concerned. When asked if she was all right, she just said everything was fine. The idea of incest or parental abuse was not a subject the school wanted to address during that time period.

Maureen was almost a grown woman before she finally left her home. Her mother had passed away and her father's abuse became more frequent and much more threatening. He had started drinking more after his wife's death. Maureen finally knew it was time to leave him and have her own life.

She did not have boyfriends during high school. She did not have any friends with the girls. Being the subject of her father's abuse for so long she was afraid of getting close to people.

When she met Joseph while working at the diner, he treated her like she was the most beautiful woman in the world. He always left her a very nice tip and when he started arriving at closing time to give her a ride to her apartment, it seemed natural for her to start having an affair with him. He would tell her about his wife and children. He told her about his important position at the hospital. She knew he was under a great deal of stress and had no trouble catering to his every whim.

He would bring her small gifts when he visited. He brought her flowers a few times which gave her such joy. Those evenings she would be expected to perform in ways that she found repulsive. Then she knew if she fulfilled his every desire, he would love her more than his wife and be hers someday.

The last night they spent together had been especially demanding of her. Joseph seemed to be insatiable with his desire of her body. When they lay together when he had finished, she brought up the question of his leaving Abby to be with her.

When he became angry, she was shocked. She told him she thought that was what he wanted. He stood up and started dressing. All the while he spoke to her in a way she had never expected. He told her if she ever thought he would leave his respectable family for her and her bastard son, she was crazier than he already thought. He told her he was a very important person at the hospital and the scandal would ruin his career.

After he walked out of her small apartment, she could not believe what had happened. She decided at that time, her future would be very different from what she had planned.

She decided to take care of Joseph. She knew if she could not have him in her life, neither could Abby. Her father had taught her all about servicing a car. She found it very simple to cut the brake line on Joseph's car. He always parked in the same space at the hospital. She waited until dark and no one noticed her near his vehicle. She did not cut through the entire line, but enough that it would break someplace before he reached home.

She waited for him to leave and followed in her small car. As the highway became more congested, she speeded up to keep his car in sight. When he tried to stop at an intersection on the heavily travelled road, his brakes failed. She came to a stop far enough away and watched as his car careened ahead into a large truck coming the other way. When he crashed, his car burst into flames.

Maureen sat in her car for quite some time before driving home. She felt no remorse. Only gratification for her actions. She saw her father's face in the flames of Joseph's car and felt pleased that she had ended the years of humiliation at his hands.

She drove home and did not say a word to anyone about what she had done. She saw a report of the accident on television. The police said it was an accident which took the life of Joseph Sampson. They showed a photo of him with Abby and their children. She poured herself a glass of wine and sat drinking without shedding a tear.

Now it appeared her talents would be used again to dispose of Abby.

She would wait until Abby had been told about Joe's lies to her and the family. Then she would end the only person standing in her way of a secure future.

CHAPTER TWENTY-FIVE:

Joe climbed the stairs to his loft apartment over the garage. He sat on the bed thinking about his failed attempt to change Maureen's plans. He was not sure what his next move should be. He loved his mother but could not stand beside her as she hurt Abby. He knew the truth had to come out, but he was not ready to ruin his life with Abby and Shawn.

He was surprised when the tears started. He had not cried since he was a boy. He had become hardened during his life with Maureen. He had not shed a tear when Joseph died. His mother had tried to comfort him with plans for their life. He believed her when she told him about money they should be getting from Joseph. When that did not happen, she began to plan for their future in other ways.

He had not met Abby and he had always done as his mother asked. Now that had all changed. Abby and Shawn had taken him into their home on that rainy night weeks ago. They had given him food and a place to live. He had a good job working at the shop.

He had a family. Siblings who had shown him acceptance. He did not believe it had all been an act. He enjoyed the feeling of love. They did not look at him as a bastard child of their father. He refused to believe Maureen when she said they would all turn on him when they heard the truth.

He looked out the window and saw the lights shining in the house. He wanted to go to Abby and Shawn and tell them everything. He was afraid of their reaction, but he knew he would try to make them understand. He had to for his future and for their safety.

*****

Shawn watched Joe as he walked into the driveway. "Joe is home," he said to Abby. "Are you going over to talk to him now?" she asked. He walked over and sat down on the sofa next to her. "I think it can wait until tomorrow." He leaned over and kissed her before he went back to the newspaper he had been reading.

"I wonder if he ate any dinner." Shawn looked at her and smiled. "He is a grown man my dear. I think he can get a meal for himself. If he is hungry, he will come over to check for leftovers." Abby laughed. "Yes, you are right. I always worry about my children too much even now that they are all grown up."

They sat quietly reading and looked up when Joe came in the front door. "Hi." He said as he saw them in the den. Shawn nodded and waited for Abby to question him about eating. When she did just that he started to laugh. Abby gave him a playful poke in the ribs.

Joe smiled and told them he had gotten a sandwich at the deli. Even though it was a small fib, it did not seem important. He sat down on the floor next to Nutmeg. The cat rubbed on his hand as Joe smoothed his fur.

Shawn noticed the strange look on Joe's face. He made no comment but waited for the boy to speak. He did not understand why he had a feeling of dread. When Joe looked up them, he knew something was about to happen that would upset their lives.

Joe looked at Shawn and Abby and took a deep breath. He was not prepared for what he had to tell them. He decided not to wait any longer. He was worried about what Maureen might do next. He had to prevent them from being hurt regardless of the consequences to him.

Abby looked over at Joe. "Joe? Is everything all right?" He hesitated before he answered her. "No Abby. I am afraid it is far from all right. I have something to tell you both. I do not want to, but it is necessary before anything bad happens."

Shawn put his paper down. "Does it have anything to do with that woman I saw you talking to this morning?" Joe was not aware that Shawn had seen him with Maureen. "Yes, it does." They waited for him to continue. Shawn saw how upset Joe looked. "Who is she?" he asked. Joe looked at him and forced himself to answer the question. "She is my mother, Maureen."

Abby gasped when she heard Joe's words. She looked at Shawn. She saw his face change from concern to anger. "Your mother Joe? You told us she had died." Shawn stood up and moved towards Joe. Abby shouted at him. "Please Shawn. Let him explain."

Shawn turned and walked back to the sofa. He sat down by her side and waited for Joe's explanation. As the boy spoke and told them everything, neither of them made any comments. He told about the plan that Maureen had come up with months before. Even the threats that she was making about Abby.

"I could not wait for her to harm you, Abby. I will understand if you hate me and want me to leave. I promise to never bother either of you again. I just want you both safe. I am so sorry for all of it."

Abby looked at Shawn before she went to Joe. She pulled him up and put her arms around him. Shawn tried to control his feelings when he saw her reaction to Joe's story. He wanted to grab Joe and throw him out of the house but waited before he acted.

"Joe. I do not want you to leave our home. Please make me understand why your mother would want to hurt me. What does she think she will gain by her actions?" Joe told them about her idea for getting Abby to change her will and make him the sole heir of her money. He said Maureen felt the money should have come to them from his father's will. He tried to explain how desperate his mother had become after the money had stopped. He said Joseph had supported them and when he died the money was not there to pay the rent or buy food. The job Maureen had was not good enough to support them. He told about how they had to move and only had a small room in a motel.

"How could she as a mother really think I would turn my back on my children. After Shawn and I marry, we had plans of making new wills. They would include you and Cassie and Henry as our beneficiaries. We had discussed the fact that we wanted you to remain living over the garage for as long as you wanted. Also, the job at the antique shop was yours for however long you chose to remain." She looked at Shawn and knew how angry he was, but she also knew he cared about Joe and would control his anger.

Abby continued, "I do agree with your mother about one thing. I feel your father should have left provision for you in his will as his son. I am sure if he had lived longer, he would have done just that. He may not have always been faithful to me, but he always supported his children."

Joe found it hard to say anything. He glanced at Shawn and expected him to start punching at any moment. He remembered how he had told Joe from the beginning to not ever hurt Abby. Now he had done just that. He heard Abby's words but found it difficult to believe them. How could she possibly forgive him for the deception?

CHAPTER TWENTY-SIX:

Shawn sat next to Abby trying to control his anger. He heard Joe's explanation about Maureen. He watched his face as he spoke. Abby believed his story and he was trying hard to do the same.

When Shawn finally started speaking, Joe expected the worst. "Joe. I have heard everything you said. I want to believe your story for Abby's sake. You know I warned you from the beginning. I have a strong urge to give you a beating before throwing you into the street.

Joe listened and felt like he should be prepared for Shawn's actions. When he looked up at Shawn, he saw something he had been afraid to hope for. Shawn stood next to Abby, and they were both smiling at him. Abby stretched out her arms and took Joe into her embrace. Shawn patted him on the back and told him they would work everything out, together as a family.

"I am willing to follow Abby's lead with you Joe. I do believe in giving a second chance when it is deserved. You have proven to us during your time here that you can be a responsible young man. I have seen you with Abby and with her children. I felt the sincerity of your words when you spoke about your mother. You have lived a hard life with her and sometimes our own thoughts of right and wrong can be changed when we listen to stronger more forceful people."

Abby listened to Shawn with a feeling of pride for the man she was about to take as her husband. Shawn continued, "I am not sure how we are going to address this problem, but we will find a solution. I will add one other thing. Joe, if I find out you are still deceiving us, I promise you will pay for it in a very painful and life changing way."

Joe looked at Shawn's outstretched hand. He took it in his. "I do not know how to thank you both. I promise I am telling you the truth now. I will do anything you want that will solve the problem with my mother. She must be made to understand this craziness has to end."

Shawn agreed and looked at Abby as he shook Joe's hand. She did not speak aloud but mouthed her words. "Thank You."

Abby went to the kitchen to make coffee while Shawn talked to Joe in the den. She could hear their low voices but could not make out what they were saying. She quickly pushed away the tears that rolled down her cheek.

Abby felt worried about exactly what actions Maureen was willing to take. She tried to understand the woman's panic at her financial situation. If Maureen would listen to her, she could explain about changing the will to include Joe. She even considered helping Maureen get set up in a suitable living arrangement. Perhaps she could help her find employment that would help her.

She would listen to any decision Shawn had produced to manage the situation. She had every confidence in his ability to keep her and the rest of the family safe from harm.

As she poured the coffee, she stopped when she realized she would have to explain to Cassie and Henry about Joe and his mother. She hoped they would be able to forgive him as she had.

Abby carried the tray into the den. She told Shawn and Joe that she had decided to wait until morning before calling her children. "With Cassie being pregnant I do not want to upset her any more than necessary." Shawn agreed that was a good idea. "If my children are as loving as I think, they will consider your situation Joe. They had a childhood that was so different from yours. It might be difficult for them at first, but I have a feeling they will both come around to understanding the struggles you have had with your mother."

CHAPTER TWENTY-SEVEN:

Joe woke the next morning early. He saw that the sun had not risen. He lay on his bed thinking about the talk with Abby and Shawn. They had listened to his explanation and still seemed to be behind him. He did not look forward to the phone call with his siblings. He would not be surprised to hear they did not want any more to do with him after his deception about his mother.

Abby woke before the alarm sounded. She thought about the phone call she needed to make to her children. She hoped she could convince them to understand Joe's explanation as to his deception about his mother. She knew her daughter Cassie would be more prone to acceptance than Henry would.

Shawn rolled over and saw that she was awake. "Good morning. I see that serious frown. Thinking about the call you must make today?" She nodded and leaned over to kiss him. "Yes, I really do not look forward to calling either Cassie or Henry. They both took to Joe so easily. I really hate to destroy that compassion they showed him."

He watched as she got out of the bed. She pulled on her robe and told him she would put the coffee on. "Get some more sleep if you want. It is still early. I will be downstairs."

Shawn waited a few minutes. He too was concerned about having to explain to Cassie and Henry. He had a feeling their response was not going to be what anyone expected.

He had no plan as to managing the problem with Maureen. From what Joe had said it did not seem she would be someone who would listen to reason. His own opinion was that she had gone over the edge regarding her delusion about Joseph and the truth. He doubted she would listen to anything either of them could say to her. He considered going to the local authorities, but no crime had been committed. Besides, he did not want to get Joe in trouble with the police. He had a juvenile record which should not be public knowledge and he would rather keep it that way.

Abby looked up as Shawn came into the kitchen. "Decided to join me I see." She said as she handed him a cup of coffee. "Yes, I did not want you stressing by yourself." She sat next to him at the table. "What do you really think about the situation? Do you have any idea of how we should respond to Maureen?"

Shawn looked at her and smiled. "You want the truth?" Abby nodded. "Well, personally I think Joe's mother belongs in the local loony bin. She has no sense of reality. She sounds like she really believed that Joseph was leaving you and the children to make a life with her and Joe. From what you have told me, I find that to be something that had never crossed his mind."

Abby thought about his comment. "I have gone over the last few years of our marriage so many times in my mind. I knew he missed being home with the children while they were growing up. He never showed any signs of being dissatisfied with our marriage. Whenever he could be home with us, he was always a loving husband to me and a good father to the kids. Our sexual life never changed. He did not spend a lot of time seeing to my satisfaction, but he always seemed content himself with our love making. Maybe there were things he needed that I did not give to him. If I had been different maybe, he would never have turned to another woman in the first place."

Shawn reached out and took her hand. "OK. Now that is the last time, I want to hear that statement. You are the most loving and giving woman I have ever met. You give yourself freely and totally. You please me in every possible way. Both in bed and out. I cannot imagine that you could have done anything to keep your husband from straying to another. Some men just need more."

Abby smiled when she heard his words. "Thank you, Shawn. I love you so much. You really do not deserve all this baggage." Without another word he stood and pulled her into his arms. His kiss told her how much he loved her. "What I do not deserve is a woman as special as you. I am just an old angler who stumbled into your shop one day. You took me under your wing and turned me into a much better man. I plan on spending the rest of my life trying to be worthy of you."

When Abby looked up at him, she had tears in her eyes. Shawn saw Joe standing in the kitchen doorway. He looked like he was ready to cry also. "Hey there kiddo. I see you could not sleep either." He said to the boy who was trying to keep from joining Abby in her tears.

Abby wiped her eyes and looked around. "Good morning, Joe." She went to the counter and poured his coffee. The three sat down at the table and sat drinking their coffee without speaking.

Finally, Joe looked up at them. "Sorry I interrupted you before. I heard the words you were saying to Abby. I never remember my father talking like that to my mother. I do agree with you Shawn. I have come to believe my mother is delusional in her thinking."

Abby reached over and touched Joe's hand. "We are going to come up with a solution to this problem. Have faith Joe." He nodded but had a feeling there would be no persuading his mother to change her way of thinking about Abby.

CHAPTER TWENTY-EIGHT:

Abby waited while the phone dialed Cassie's number. "Mom? Good morning. Is everything all right?" Abby took a breath. "Good morning sweetie. Sorry to be calling so early. I wanted to catch you before you left for work."

Joe watched as Abby take a deep breath and continued with her call. "We are all fine here. How about you? How are you feeling?" Cassie responded with a brief description of her pregnancy. "The babies are both doing fine. Now tell me what is wrong. I can hear something in your voice."

Abby glanced at Shawn and Joe. It seemed like neither of them were breathing. "Yes, there is some news that I must share with you and your brother. It might be upsetting to hear, but please try to listen with an open mind and heart." She continued to explain about Joe and his mother. Cassie remained silent, but Abby could hear her breathing as it changed. "I understand if this is alarming to you. Specially to hear your father had another family besides you and Henry." She waited for Cassie to speak. After what seemed like minutes, she heard her daughter's response.

"Mom? Are you all right with this confession from Joe? Do you believe him?" Abby told her that it did take her time to process his words. "I must admit I was shocked to hear his mother was in fact alive. I heard him explain about their home and how he was raised. I know your father loved you and Henry very much. I was angry at first to think he could have had another woman and son. But, since we have lived under the same roof with Joe, I have come to understand what a good person he truly is underneath." "I do feel sorry for the way he had to grow up. Henry and I both felt protective of him when we met. We may not have had dad around all the time, but we still had more of a happy childhood than Joe had. I am trying to understand why he chose to deceive us. I know it sounds like his mother has quite a lot of control over him. However, he has come to know you and I am sure he sees the loving and compassionate woman you are. What about his mother? Have you had any contact with her since the truth has come out?"

Abby told her it had only been a day and they had not decided how to proceed with Maureen. "Shawn and I are trying to be as understanding as possible." Cassie asked what Shawn's reaction was to hear the truth from Joe. "Well, at first, I thought I would have to physically get between the two of them. Shawn has calmed down since Joe first told us the truth. He thinks Maureen is a serious threat to all of us. We feel we should go ahead with caution."

Cassie agreed that sounded like a wise decision. "What about notifying the police?" she asked. "There has been no real crime committed. We want to try to prevent anything physical happening to any of us." Cassie asked if she wanted her to call Henry. "Thank you dear. This is something he must hear from me personally." Cassie said she understood. She asked Abby if she and Jake should come. "No. I do not want you or your family any closer to possible danger. I will tell Henry the same when I speak to him. Just please take care of yourself. I do not want this to upset you or cause any problems with the babies."

After a few more encouraging words, Abby hung up the call. She looked at Joe whose face showed how worried he was feeling. "It will be all right Joe. Cassie is strong. She will be able to process this news and I am sure in time; she will be behind you one hundred percent."

Joe managed a small grin and nodded. "Are you going to call Henry?" he asked her. "Yes, we might as well get it over with sooner than later. Why don't you take Nutmeg outside and wait on the patio?" Shawn agreed with her and stood to open the door. Nutmeg walked outside and sat in the sunshine. Joe joined the cat and they walked towards the back yard together.

Shawn looked at Abby. "Are you all right? How did Cassie respond to the news?" Abby tried to control her emotions as she told him what Cassie had said. "She offered to come but I did not think that was advisable under the circumstances." He agreed. He did not want any more people involved that would need protection from anything Maureen might have planned.

After refreshing her coffee, Abby dialed Henry's phone. It rang quite a few times before she heard his voice. "Mom? What's wrong? Why are you calling so early?" She took a moment and went ahead with a similar explanation to Cassie's phone call. She was surprised that Henry did not interrupt her but waited til she was finished speaking.

"Henry? Are you still on the line?" she asked. "Yes mom. I am still here. I cannot believe that Joe lied to you about his mother being dead. I have to say I was really impressed with him when we met. It took me a few minutes to accept what dad had done to all of us. Cassie and I both agreed that it was not Joe's fault for being born and that we should not hold any grudge against him. However, to find out he has been lying to you and all of us for weeks really has me wondering. I know you are ready to forgive him. I could hear that in your voice. It might take us longer to come to that decision."

Abby listened to her son and felt relieved that he had not shown more anger towards Joe. "Mom, is Shawn there with you?" Abby said that he was. "Can I speak to him? Privately, please?" Abby looked at Shawn. "Henry wants to speak to you. Alone." She handed him the phone and walked out of the room.

"Hello Henry." Shawn said. "Hi Shawn. All right I listened to mom's explanation. Now I want to hear your opinion. I trust your judgement. Especially when it comes to mom's safety. Are you worried about Joe's mother? Do you think she is a real threat?"

Shawn told Henry exactly what his first reaction was. He told him that Abby had stopped him from becoming physical with Joe. "I tried very hard to hear Joe while he explained about his mother and her plan. I agree with you. It is serious. Maureen sounds like an unstable woman who does pose a threat to your mother. Trust me when I say that I will not let anything happen to hurt Abby. I love her with my whole heart, and I would lay down my life to save hers."

"Thanks for your honesty, Shawn. I know how much you love mom. We all saw and heard your proposal to her. Will you promise me one thing? If the situation starts to go south, you will notify the police and let them handle Maureen." Shawn agreed with Henry. They spoke for a short time and Henry said to keep Abby safe. Then he hung up.

Shawn joined Abby in the den. She saw how serious his face looked. "Well? What did Henry have to say?" Shawn explained what Henry had said on the phone. He told her that her son's main concern was her safety. "I told him I would make sure nothing bad happened to you or anyone else."

She walked over to him, and he put his arms around her. They were standing in each other's arms when Joe appeared in the door. He smiled when he saw them. "Is everything all right?" he asked.

Shawn reached out his arm towards Joe. "Come hear kid. We have plenty of this to go around." Joe walked over to Shawn and they both grabbed the boy for a huge embrace. "It is going to be all right Joe. We are going to make sure of that," Shawn told him.

CHAPTER TWENTY-NINE:

Cassie had just finished with explaining to Jake about Joe. She was not surprised when she saw her brother's ID on the ringing phone. "Hi Henry. I was expecting your call. I imagine you heard from mom?" He said he had. "Sis, what do you think? Do you buy this story from Joe? I know mom does, but after talking to Shawn I must admit I am worried about what happens next."

Cassie told Henry she was still processing the entire story. She agreed with him about worrying what Maureen's next move could be. "I offered to go home, but Mom said she did not want to put any of us in danger. I think she is more worried than she wants to admit." He agreed. "Listen sis, you have to take care of yourself. This pregnancy has been good so far. Please keep it that way. I am sure if Shawn feels we should come home, he will call."

They spoke for quite some time before Cassie ended the call. Jake sat next to her and watched his wife closely. "Are you sure you are all right?" he asked. "I know you are worried about your mom, but you have to promise to take care of yourself." He said as he put his hand over her growing stomach. "I do not want you to put yourself or our little one in any more stress than you have to."

Cassie smiled at her husband. She leaned over and kissed him deeply. "I love you so much. You are the best thing that ever happened to me. I have no intention of putting myself or this little bundle in any danger. I am worried about mom and Shawn. I know he will keep her safe in any situation. I just hope nothing happens beyond his control."

*****

Abby and Shawn spent the morning talking to Joe about his mother. Shawn wanted him to tell them everything that Maureen had said about her plan to eliminate Abby. Joe knew how much Shawn cared about Abby and he hoped he could protect her.

Abby finally announced that she felt they should go into town and open the shop. "We need a diversion right now. I think we will be safer closer to people in town. Maureen will not try anything when there are so many witnesses around."

Shawn agreed and after they got changed, they drove into the shop. Abby had left Nutmeg outside on the patio as usual for the day. When they drove out of the drive, no one noticed Maureen watching from the side of the garage. She waited until they were gone before she walked over to the kitchen door. The car jack in her hand made fast work on the back door. She looked around the room as she entered.

Maureen walked and looked in every room of the house. She smashed all she could to destroy anything Abby held dear. Upstairs in the bedrooms, she pulled clothing from the closets. Using the kitchen knife, she had found, she ripped through the material easily. Throwing the ruined clothes on the floor, she took the knife to the bedding. Feathers flew everywhere as she tore through the bed pillows. The mattress lay in pieces when she was finished.

She threw perfume bottles at the mirror over the dresser. Glass flew in pieces on the floor. She went in the bathroom and turned on the water in the sink and the tub. As the levels rose, she started to laugh. Pleased with her progress, she went downstairs again.

Walking into the den, she looked around at the cozy setting. "This should have all been mine." She thought. She went to the fireplace and started a fire. Throwing more paper than necessary into the blaze she watched as the flames leaped out into the room.

Feeling satisfied with her destruction she walked into the kitchen again. Looking in the refrigerator she helped herself to some left-over food. When she noticed Nutmeg sitting outside on the patio, she started towards the door. As she pulled the door open, the cat jumped up. When he did not recognize the crazed woman in the doorway, he ran for cover in the back yard.

Leaving the door hanging open, Maureen walked away from the house as the flames leaped higher. She laughed as she made her way from the back yard. "If I cannot have that home, that bitch cannot either."

CHAPTER THIRTY:

Shawn was helping a customer when he saw the firetrucks fly down the street. He did not think anything except worry for whatever danger they were heading towards.

Abby sat in the office preparing the deposit when the phone rang. " Mrs. Sampson? This is Muriel Evans. I live next door to you. Your house is on fire dear. I did not know if you were aware. I am so sorry to have to give you bad news."

Abby jumped up from her desk. She ran towards Shawn yelling. "Shawn the house is on fire. The woman next door just called me." The customers looked startled and said they would come back. Shawn grabbed his keys and called for Joe who was in the back room. The three ran out of the store and rushed to their car.

As Shawn got closer to the house, they could see multiple fire trucks in the street and the driveway. He parked nearby and Abby started to run towards the house. Joe followed and stopped short behind her. They stood looking at the house which was fully engulfed in flames. The firemen had their hoses aimed at the fire but did not seem to be making any headway.

Shawn stood with his arm around Abby. The tears ran down her face as she watched her beautiful home being destroyed by the fire. Suddenly she pulled away from Shawn. "Where are you going? It is not safe." Abby ran to the back yard. The firefighters ran toward her before she could get any closer to the house. "Ma'am. It is not safe. Please stay back."

Abby screamed. "I am looking for my cat. Nutmeg, where are you?" Shawn and Joe caught up with her as the firefighter was leading her back to the driveway. She looked up at Shawn. "Oh, Shawn. Where is

Nutmeg? I left him out back when we left." Before he could answer her question, he saw a woman walking towards them.

Abby looked up and saw Muriel walking toward her. In her arms, was a frightened but safe Nutmeg. "Abby, he was hiding on my back porch. I recognized him as your cat. He is fine. Just scared." She looked at the burning house. Abby took Nutmeg in her arms and cried. "Oh Nutmeg. I am so glad you are not hurt." Joe reached for the cat and stood holding him tightly.

Shawn looked towards the garage. "Well, Joe. Looks like we all might be roommates for a while." He said as he saw that the garage appeared undamaged from the blaze. Joe smiled. "Fine by me."

The three stood for hours and watched as the fire took the beautiful house to a pile of burnt wood on the ground. The fire chief walked over and spoke quietly to Shawn. "He asked if we had left the fireplace going when we left for the shop. I told him that we had not. Then he said they saw that the house appeared to be ransacked before the fire started." Abby looked at him.

Shawn nodded in response to her silent question. He only uttered one word. "Maureen"

CHAPTER THIRTY-ONE:

Abby stood with Shawn watching as the firefighters worked on the fire. She could not believe her beautiful home was now a pile of smoldering wood. The few pieces of furniture that could be salvaged sat on the lawn.

Joe glanced at Abby and could not begin to understand how his mother could do such a thing. They had not even mentioned Maureen's name to him, but he knew their thoughts were the same. He felt a growing rage directed at his mother.

Shawn saw the look on Joe's face. He reached over for the boy and pressed his arm. "It will be all right Joe. We are all safe. Nutmeg was not hurt." Before he could continue, Abby spoke. "It is just a house Joe. It can be replaced. If we are all right, that is what is important. I am not going to let your mother take away what feelings we have for each other."

Hours passed and Shawn convinced Abby to go up to the loft apartment and rest. He stood with Joe as the firefighters cleared their hoses from around the property. The fire chief had told Shawn the fire inspectors would be in touch after their investigation was ended.

Joe looked up at Shawn. "I know you and Abby are thinking that my mother did this horrible thing. I must admit that is my opinion also. I am so sorry for bringing all this into your lives." Shawn put his arm around the boy's shoulder. They walked up the stairs to the loft together. Abby was sitting at the small table when they entered.

"Did the fire chief have any further information?" she asked Shawn. "No. They will contact us when they know anything further." He replied. "Shawn. What are we going to do now? Maureen seems to be determined to punish me for Joseph's shortcomings. Maybe it is time to involve the police." Shawn sat down across from Abby while Joe took a spot on the bed. "We should wait for the report about the fire before we talk to the police. They will probably be notified if the investigators find anything suspicious."

Abby looked at the two men. "We all need showers and some clean clothes." Shawn agreed. He said it would probably be a good idea to check into the local hotel. "We really should not stay here tonight. Just in case Maureen returns. Do you think Muriel will take care of Nutmeg for us?" Abby took her phone and after speaking to the neighbor she told Shawn they could bring Nutmeg on their way into town. "I will feel better knowing he is safe while we are gone," she told him.

After they dropped the cat at the neighbor's house, they drove into town. Shawn had called ahead and booked them rooms in the hotel. They stopped at the local department store and bought new clothes. As they settled into the hotel, Abby walked into the bathroom to shower. She stood under the running water finally releasing the tears that she had been holding back for hours.

"How could her life turn from perfect to a disaster in only days?" When she finally came out of the bathroom, she had composed herself. Shawn could tell that she had been crying but did not comment. He watched as she dressed and when he was satisfied that she was all right, he took his turn under the hot water.

Shawn was upset with Maureen too. However, his feelings were not sadness. He felt a growing rage inside that he was having trouble controlling. The woman he loved more than anything was in danger from a deranged person. He vowed to keep her safe no matter what happened.

When Shawn came out of the bathroom, he had decided. "I am going to contact the police. I am concerned that Maureen may try to destroy the antique shop. I hope they can have security watch the shop tonight to make sure it is safe." Abby agreed with his idea. The thought had crossed her mind also.

*****

Maureen had arrived back at the motel after the fire. She felt gratification for her act of revenge against Abby. "Now that bitch has no home. Just like me. Too bad I could not catch that stupid cat. I would have broken its neck and left it for her to find." She smiled to herself about her evil thoughts.

"They think this fire is the worst thing to happen. They have no idea what is coming. They will all regret the day they ever opened the door to Joe. Her kids will hate him as much as that woman will in the days to come. He will come back to me thankful that his mother is the only person who cares about him." She thought while sitting in the dark of the motel room.

CHAPTER THIRTY-TWO:

Abby sat in the hotel watching the news. She opened the door to find Joe standing in the hall outside. "Are you feeling better?" he asked her. "Yes. Joe. I am fine. Come in." He walked inside and heard Shawn on the phone with the police.

"They will have a patrol car stationed near the shop overnight. Just in case Maureen decides to do more damage. I told them where she was staying, and they are sending officers to the motel." Joe nodded without commenting.

Abby said she was certain they would take care of the problem. "I am hungry. Why don't we go down to the dining room and have something to eat?" The men both agreed that their stomachs were empty as well.

Joe followed as they stepped into the elevator. Abby smiled as she reached over and removed the tag from the boy's shirt. He blushed with embarrassment. "Guess I have not had too many new clothes lately. Forgot to look for tags." Shawn laughed and roughed up the boy's hair as they walked into the dining room.

The food seemed to make them all feel better. As they sat enjoying their meal, Shawn's phone rang. He told Abby the police had checked the motel room but found it empty. "They said it looked like she had checked out already." He saw the look of concern on her face.

"She probably got worried after setting the fire and left town. I have a feeling we will not hear from her again." He tried to convince Abby even though he really did not believe it himself.

Maureen sat in her car and watched as the police searched her motel room. She had decided to leave only minutes before the squad car arrived in the parking lot. They had not noticed her car that was parked around the edge of the building.

She thought it would be smart to leave town. At least for a few days. She needed time to plan her next move towards Abby. She had decided to confront her before she ended her life. She wanted the satisfaction of seeing Abby's face when she faced death.

Sleeping in her car overnight proved to be uncomfortable. However, it was satisfying to know she had destroyed Abby's house and all her memories. Now she had nothing. Only her man. Time would take him away also.

*****

After they returned from dinner, Abby decided to call Cassie and Henry to tell them about the fire. She did not want them to hear from anyone else. Their responses were the same. Shock and concern for her safety. Henry said he would leave his wife and children home and drive to Cobble Bay the next day. Abby was finally able to convince him to stay home and wait until she called him. He agreed unhappily to his mother's suggestion. "Please promise to call me if anything else happens." He told her before they ended their call.

Abby wondered about Joe. She hoped he would be able to sleep. She knew how upset he was to think his mother could be so vicious. The next day she planned on having a long talk with him about his future. She wanted to make him know just how important he had become to her and Shawn.

Abby and Shawn spent the evening in their hotel room. They tried their best to find sleep, but it proved impossible. As soon as Abby closed her eyes, all she could see was the house in flames. She had called Muriel to check on Nutmeg. Her neighbor said he was just fine. Enjoying being pampered like an honored guest in her house.

Abby tried not to think about all the photos she had lost in the fire. It almost seemed like her children's childhood had been swept away with the flames. She still had photos on her phone which made her happy to look through.

She knew she would be able to make new memories and photos with her children and grandchildren. She still had her future with Shawn and Joe. She was going to do everything possible to make certain that happened.

CHAPTER THIRTY-THREE:

Abby woke the next morning feeling like she had just fallen asleep. She heard Shawn talking quietly on the phone when she came out of the bedroom. "Good morning." He said after he had hung up his call.

"Morning to you. Who were you talking to so early?" He laughed at her question. "Early? It is almost noon. That was the fire inspector. They decided the fire was arson. With the state of the house when they arrived, it looked like someone broke in by smashing the back door."

"Did you give them Maureen's name?" Shawn nodded. "Yes, I explained the situation and he said he would give his report to the police. It is in their hands now." She saw the tray from room service and poured a cup of coffee. "Sorry I slept so late. Have you spoken to Joe this morning?" Shawn said he had met Joe downstairs for breakfast. They knew how exhausted she was and decided to let her sleep as long as she could. "Thank you." She told him.

"If you are up to it, I thought we should probably open the shop for a few hours." She agreed and finished her coffee. "I will take a quick shower and be ready to go." Shawn told her that he would call Joe and they would wait in the lobby for her.

Abby dressed as fast as she could. She was anxious to get to the antique shop to make sure everything was all right. Shawn said he had not heard anything from the police who were at the shop. She hoped that was a good sign that Maureen had done her damage and decided to move on.

Joe saw her as she came out of the elevator. "Morning Abby. Glad that you were able to rest." He said as he walked over with Shawn. "How about you Joe? Were you able to sleep at all?" He nodded as they walked outside to the parking lot. The drive to the shop only took minutes. Abby was worried they would find more damage to the shop but was pleased to see everything looked normal.

Shawn stopped to speak to the police who were sitting outside in their squad car. They told him all had been quiet. He looked around the street after they drove away. He almost wished he would see Maureen. He would love to tell her exactly how delusional she was.

Shawn took Joe to the back room and showed him the chore he had for him. When he joined Abby in the office, she was sitting staring at the bank deposit. "Are you ok?" he asked. She nodded. "Yes. I am just trying to concentrate on work. I am going to walk over to the bank."

He kissed her on the cheek as he walked her to the front door. "Maybe we will be busy enough for us both to forget about the fire." She said as she walked outside. Shawn watched her cross the street and checked to make sure no one was following her.

Joe walked into the showroom after she had left. "Did you tell her about Henry's phone call this morning?" Shawn told him no, he had not wanted to upset her. "You know she will be upset when he shows up with Cassie." Shawn said he knew exactly how she was going to react to their visit. "They are her children, and they are concerned about her. How could I tell them to stay home? Whether she admits it or not, I know she needs them both right now." Joe agreed and went back to his cleaning.

Just as a customer came into the shop, he spotted Abby coming back from the bank. She walked in and greeted the customer by name. "Good to see you today. We will be right with you. Please look around while you are waiting." She motioned to Shawn to join her in the office. "While I was in the bank, the manager took me aside. He told me a woman had been in earlier asking about the shop. He said it sounded like she was interested in buying."

Shawn was surprised. "Are you thinking of giving up the shop? I thought it meant something to you." Abby said she had no intention to sell. She was curious about who this woman was though. "Do you think it might have been Maureen looking for information?"

She left Shawn wondering while she went to help the customer. Shawn thought about calling the bank manager to get a description of the woman. Before he had the opportunity another couple entered the shop and he walked out to greet them.

The afternoon moved along with a few very good sales. There was enough business to keep them going without any spare time for their thoughts. Joe finished his job and was cleaning the break room when Shawn came in and said it was quitting time.

As they walked outside, Shawn spotted the patrol car that had just pulled up in front of the shop. He spoke to the officers and then joined Joe and Abby in their car. As they drove to the hotel, he considered telling Abby about Cassie and Henry's arrival.

When he decided to not say anything, he told her he had put a quick call in to the bank and spoke to the manager. "I got a description of the woman who was inquiring about the shop. It did not fit the woman I had seen speaking to Joe." Joe heard his comment but said nothing. He knew his mother had not given up on her plan for revenge. He also knew he would be on the look-out for her at the hotel and at the shop. He would not allow her to hurt anyone no matter what he had to do to prevent it.

After a light dinner in the hotel, they went upstairs and retired for the evening. Joe sat in his room thinking about Maureen. He had tried to call her but only got her voice mail. He told her she should stay away since the police knew she was the one who had set fire to the house. He hoped she would heed his advice, but he knew how determined she was.

Abby and Shawn watched television from their bedroom. Shawn knew she was not really watching but just pretending to keep his mind at ease. He leaned over and kissed her. "Why are you pretending when you know you hate this movie." He asked. She looked at him and smiled. "Maybe we should talk." He took the control and turned off the television.

"Do you think I should have allowed Henry to come here? I know how concerned he is with the situation." Shawn waited before answering. "Well, I guess I must come clean. Henry called me this morning while you were sleeping. He is driving to pick up Cassie and they should be here tomorrow. Please don't be angry with me. I know you need your children right now even if you try to deny it."

Abby looked at him and he could see the tears in her eyes. "Shawn, you know me so well. No, I am not mad at you. I really do need to see them, but I did not want to put them in danger. Thank you for knowing what is best for me even if I don't know myself." She kissed him and he took her in his arms. They lay together quietly until they both drifted off.

CHAPTER THIRTY-FOUR:

Abby woke and looked at the alarm clock. She was pleased to see it was still early. She felt more rested and found her appetite had returned. When she came out of the bathroom, Shawn was already dressing for the day. "I called Joe and he is downstairs in the dining room waiting for us."

They came out of the elevator arm in arm and walked into the dining room. Joe smiled when he saw Abby looking more relaxed. "Good morning you two. I ordered coffee for us." They sat and gave the waiter their order when he arrived with the coffee.

Joe looked at Shawn and he saw the wink he gave back. "Joe was worried that you would be upset with me about Henry's decision. I told him you needed all your children around now." She smiled and nodded at Shawn's comment.

"Yes, I certainly can use all my family right now." She reached over and took Joe's hand. "That includes you too." He gave a sigh of relief. "I am glad you are not mad at Shawn. He said he knew what you needed even if you would not admit it to him." They all laughed.

When they had finished breakfast, they walked back to the elevator. Joe hesitated before going to his room. "I just hope Henry and Cassie are not too disappointed with me. I might have my first big sister and brother talking to. That sounds pretty cool, if not a little scary." Abby laughed at him and went down the hall to her room.

Shawn stood in the hall with Joe. "Have you tried to call your mother?" Joe said he had a few times but had only gotten her voice mail. "Do you have any idea where she might be hiding?" Joe said he would tell him and Abby if he knew. "I want her found before she does anything else."

Shawn joined Abby in their room, convinced that Joe was telling the truth. He knew the boy was as afraid of Maureen as they were. He checked his phone for any messages from the police but found none.

When Abby freshened up, they all drove to the shop together. The routine was the same as the day before. Shawn assigned Joe jobs to do around the shop. He waited on customers while Abby took the deposit across to the bank.

The morning passed by without any incidents. A few customers had come in, but they all just seemed to be browsing. Abby checked in with her neighbor Muriel and got the report on Nutmeg. It seemed he was being cared for like the king of the house. Abby laughed when Muriel told her about feeding him canned tuna. It seemed he had quite a taste for it. She knew he was going to be spoiled by the time she could bring him home. She also knew he was safe and that gave her peace of mind.

After a light lunch at the café, they returned to the shop. Shortly after they came back to work Abby heard the bell on the shop. She looked up and was thrilled to see Cassie and Henry walking toward her.

"Oh, I am so glad to see you both. Thank you for insisting. For once, I am glad you did not do as I asked." They both grabbed her for hugs and smiled at her comment. "We could not stay away mom. I hope you did not give Shawn a bad time over our phone call." Henry said.

Shawn overheard Henry's words as he walked into the office. "Oh, brother did she. Even tried to throw a lamp at me in the hotel room." Cassie looked at her mother with a surprised expression. "Oh my gosh. Mom, you did not." Abby shook her head and laughed along with Shawn. "No, I did not. I was glad about your visit. I just did not want to put you in any danger."

Abby looked at her daughter's growing belly. "Cassie, you are really glowing. This pregnancy looks like it agrees with you." Cassie smiled. Henry turned towards her, "yeah sis. You really need to watch your weight. Getting a little pudgy in the mid-section." She reached over and poked him in the arm just as Joe walked into the office.

Both stopped talking and looked at Joe. He waited for them to speak. "Well, Joe. I think we need to have a sit down. Sibling to sibling," said Henry. Abby looked at her son. "Now Henry. Take it easy on him." Henry took Joe by the arm and started leading him into the back room while Cassie followed. "Oh, we will mom. Do not worry."

Abby started to follow them when Shawn reached out and stopped her. "Let them talk. They have to work this out by themselves. I don't think you have anything to worry about. They are your children after all." She listened to Shawn and decided to follow his orders.

They sat in the office and waited for the three to come out of the back room. "I do not hear any loud voices or breaking of glass." Shawn teased. He saw Cassie coming toward them followed by Joe and Henry. They were all smiling, and Joe looked relieved. He walked over to Abby and gave her a hug. "Thanks Abby."

"What was that for?" she asked him. "Both Cassie and Henry listened to my explanation about my mother and her crazy scheme to get back at you. They had the same reaction that you did. Even though they were slightly annoyed that I had not come forward sooner, they said they were still glad that I am their half-brother."

Abby looked at her children and nodded at them. She did not make a big statement, but just quietly mouthed the words, "I love you."

CHAPTER THIRTY-FIVE:

Shawn told Abby that he had made reservations for Cassie and Henry in the same hotel they were staying. She rode with Henry as he followed Shawn to the hotel. "I am glad you closed the shop early," Cassie said to her mother. Abby smiled, "I wanted to spend time with my two favorite children. I am so pleased that you decided to believe Joe. That young man has been through a lot with Maureen. She tried her best to corrupt his mind as a child. He finally realized when he was older that she was mentally unstable."

Henry glanced at his mother. "Does Shawn have any idea of how to manage the situation going forward?" Abby shook her head. "He said he is leaving it to the police. I wish I could believe that. When we stood watching the house go up in flames, I could see the rage on his face. He has not said anything to me, but I know he wants his chance with Maureen. I just hope the police find her first."

They parked in the hotel's parking garage and joined Shawn and Joe in the lobby. Henry got the keys to their rooms, and they all entered the elevator. Abby was glad to see their rooms were on the same floor. As they arrived at their rooms, Cassie said she wanted to rest for a short time. "Yes, please dear. You have to take care of yourself." Henry told his sister he would be with Abby. "Just come down to our room when you are ready. We can all go down for dinner together."

Henry walked with Joe. Abby watched her son as he had quiet conversation with Joe. She looked up at Shawn. "Those two surprise me every time I see them." Shawn just laughed. "Well, look at who raised them. Would you expect them to behave any other way?"

She waited while Shawn unlocked the door to their room. She knew his words were correct. She had always raised them to listen for all explanations before making judgement. She remembered that Joseph believed the same thing. He had been much more understanding when they had first met. He only got harsher and more judgmental with age.

Abby went into the bedroom while Henry and Shawn got comfortable in the living room. "How is she managing all this stress Shawn?" Henry asked. "She looks fine but seeing the house must have come as quite a shock to her." Shawn nodded. "Yes, it was hard to see her so upset. She only became totally hysterical when she thought Nutmeg was hurt. I think it was the final blow that she did not want to face. Thank goodness he had fled to the neighbor's house to hide when the fire broke out."

When Abby came back, she found them deep in conversation that stopped abruptly when they saw her enter the room. "All right. What are you two talking about?" Joe smiled and waited to see what Shawn's response was going to be. "Nothing my love. Just telling Henry how brave you have been through all the last few days."

She walked over and sat on the arm of Shawn's chair. Looking at her son and at Joe she realized there was more to the conversation but did not question him any further.

"Did you and Cassie drive by the house?" Abby asked. "Yes, we did. It is really a total loss. The only thing still standing is the garage. It looked like it was still intact. Do you have any idea of what you will do with the property?"

She looked at Shawn. "We plan to re-build, of course. There are so many memories held on that piece of land. Joe still has his loft apartment over the garage."

They were continuing their conversation about the house when Cassie appeared in the door. Abby looked up and began to speak," Cassie. I thought you were going to rest." Before she could finish Cassie walked into the room followed by Maureen who was holding a knife to her throat.

Shawn and Joe jumped up and started to approach her. "I would not come any closer," Maureen said as she looked at the two men. "Just sit back down." She pushed Cassie towards Shawn and watched as Joe stood in front of her. "They have really done a number on your brain son. I see you have ganged up with this bunch against your own mother. How could you after all I have done for you."

Joe stopped walking closer to Maureen. "All you have done. How can you say that mother? All you have ever done is fill my head with lies about Abby and her family. You have been obsessed with your plots of revenge for so long. You made me believe these people were evil. They are not. You are the evil one. You need help mother. Just put down the knife and let me help you now."

He tried to get closer, but Maureen edged herself closer to Cassie. The madness in her eyes made Abby realize she had completely lost all touch with reality. "Joe. Please. Be careful." She said to the boy.

Abby stood and started to walk toward her daughter. "Please Maureen. My daughter is pregnant. She means you no harm. Can't we all just sit down and discuss the situation rationally without anyone getting hurt any further?"

Maureen smiled at Abby. "Oh. Now the bitch wants to talk things over. Why didn't you discuss things with Joseph when he wanted to divorce you? Our entire lives could have been so different if you had just given him what he wanted. What he needed to be happy. Me."

Abby looked at the woman who again had grabbed her daughter's arm and threatened her with the knife. Cassie was trying to be calm, but Abby could see the terror on her face.

Abby ignored the others in the room. She continued to try and reason with Maureen. "I know you believe that Joseph wanted to leave me and be with you. That is not the truth. He never asked me for a divorce. Yes, we had our problems, but he still loved us. Whenever he did find time away from the hospital, he remained a good father to our children. He also stayed a loving husband to me. In every sense of the word. Never once did I have any reason to believe that he was having an affair with another woman."

Maureen listened and a strange look came over her face. For a moment she looked perfectly coherent. She bent her head. "I know that he still loved you more than me. I would never have caused his accident if I had believed he would be mine someday."

Joe looked at his mother when he heard her words. "Mom? What are you saying? You are the reason dad had that accident?" Abby gasped when she heard Maureen's story about how she had cut the brake line on Joseph's car. She looked from Cassie to Henry. They both looked as shocked and upset as she felt.

Cassie turned her head towards Maureen. "You are the reason our father died? How could you do that to someone you say you loved? You really are crazy." With her final words, Cassie pulled out of Maureen's arms. She fell on the floor near the sofa while Henry lunged for the knife in Maureen's hands.

Joe rushed to help Henry as he wrestled with Maureen. The knife fell to the floor. Joe turned toward his mother and started forward. Just as he was about to reach her Shawn pushed him aside.

Maureen backed up through the terrace doors. Shawn kept coming at her. Just as he reached out for her arm, she stumbled and fell over the railing. Abby screamed when she saw Maureen go over the railing.

Shawn looked down at Maureen's distorted body on the sidewalk ten floors below him. He looked at Joe. "I did not want that to happen. I saw she was getting too close to the railing. I tried to grab her. It all happened so fast."

Joe saw his mother's body and turned to walk back inside the room. He glanced at Shawn. "I know you were trying to save her Shawn. We all saw that. Maybe she can finally have some peace now.

Joe sat down on the sofa. The others all stood around. Each in a state of shock. Shawn picked up his phone and called 911. The police arrived shortly after his call. The detective questioned the entire group. They all told him about Maureen arriving holding a knife on Cassie. He glanced at her and seeing she was pregnant asked if she needed medical aid.

Cassie shook her head. Henry stood holding his sister. "She will be fine officer. We are all in shock over what just happened. This woman was determined to take our mother's life. She burned down our family home days ago."

Henry told him that he had managed to get the knife away from Maureen. After hearing her confession about killing their father they all tried to reason with her. She became hysterical and moved to the terrace. Joe told the officer that before Shawn could reach her, she slipped and fell over the low railing.

"My mother was a sick woman officer. She believed Abby took her lover away. She did that by tampering with his brake lines." The detective took statements from each person and the story was the same each time. He left the group after getting his information.

Abby went to Shawn. She could see how shaken he was. "We all know you tried Shawn. She was beyond hearing anyone. I am so sorry you had to go through this horrible experience. But thank you for saving my children." She told him as he took her in his arms.

EPILOGUE:

Maureen's death was declared an accident. The police had been told how she had confessed to killing Joseph. Shawn told them she had entered the hotel room extremely distraught. After her confession he reported she ran to the terrace where she slipped and fell over the edge. The others present in the room all agreed with his explanation.

Abby and Shawn watched as the builders finished the final pieces of their new house. It had turned out almost better than the original. "I cannot believe they have completed the build so fast," she told him.

"They were not going to waste any time getting the house done. They knew our timeline for the wedding was almost completed. Now we can get married on the patio and have all our family and friends. They will witness our joining and see just how much I love you." Shawn told her.

Joe walked up behind them and laughed. "Don't you two ever get tired of being so lovey, dovey?" he asked them.

Shawn reached over and tousled the boy's hair. "Not at all. Some day we will be asking you the same thing."

Joe watched Abby and Shawn as they kissed each other. He had never been so happy before. He now had a mother and father who loved him and cared for his future. His brother and sister would arrive soon with their families for the wedding.

Joe finally found his forever home in COBBLE BAY.

THE END.

www.ingramcontent.com/pod-product-compliance
Lightning Source LLC
Chambersburg PA
CBHW081914120726
47996CB00010B/3324